OUR LADY

OF THE NORTH

A BRINKER NOVEL

JAMES C. MITCHELL

Published by Rafter Five Press

Tucson, Arizona

ISBN 978-0-9673497-7-0

The Brinker Novels

by James C. Mitchell

OUR LADY OF THE NORTH

CHOKE POINT

LOVERS CROSSING

OUR LADY OF THE NORTH

A Brinker Novel

James C. Mitchell

1

Back then, when I thought of Carla Baca, I remembered a teenage woman. She had a Mexican beauty's cinnamon skin and luminous black hair and dark, knowing eyes. She dressed well, never too fancy for high school, never immodestly like many of the girls. Carla was friendly but often alone. Her quiet confidence signaled unattainability. Got the world on a string, string around her finger, but she never showed her hand. Carla's going places, we all said, and we were right.

Now that I know where she went, I remember her differently.

The North

Six exhausted travelers stole into Phoenix at a few minutes after eleven on a summer night. The child slept. The five adults stared out the van windows, hoping no *policía* looked in. They kept silent, afraid and awed. None had ever seen a place like this, except on the fantasy world of television.

The sprawling desert city pulsed with life and promise. The people in the van saw an automobile racetrack, its floodlights still blazing as crowds departed. Then came a shopping mall with twenty-four movie theatres, the sign said, and dozens of stores. Here was a grand hotel built into a hillside. Up ahead, enormous airplanes floated down to land, one after another.

A sparkling cluster of tall buildings lay to the west. *Rascacielos,* they were called in Spanish: scraping the sky. In their midst, the great baseball stadium, where boys from Mexico came legally and became dollar millionaires. Gleaming expensive cars flashed by. Young passengers in sleek convertibles laughed and waved as they sped to new pleasures in the warm desert night.

And this was only Phoenix. Imagine what Los Angeles must be like!

Then, with just a few turns, they reached another part of the city. Scary dark. No moon. The street looked abandoned and passed by. Not a light glowed in the small stucco houses. These places would be luxurious in Mexico, but the travelers sensed that this was a poor neighborhood – perhaps even dangerous – by the standards of *el norte*.

The driver turned off the van headlights and eased down the last block to a house at the end of the street. The other *coyote* jumped out and pushed up the garage door. He pulled it closed when the van had crept inside. They sat there, waiting until the guides led them into the house.

All six people were ordered into one room. There was a single bed. They agreed without discussion that Lourdes would take it. She had an eighteen-month-old daughter, Irma, with her and another child due soon. Her husband Pablo took the narrow space between the bedside and the wall, beneath a window painted black, nailed shut, and barred outside. The sounds of cars and trucks on the big highway seeped in all night. Every few minutes, jet engines rumbled overhead, not far away. Irma, undisturbed, still slept in her mother's arms.

The other three Mexicans took up positions around the room. They were two men and a woman, all unrelated. They curled into corners or kept a respectful distance on what little floor remained. Anyone who needed the toilet had to knock, be let out by a guard and escorted to the bathroom, then brought back and locked back in again.

They were hungry. They smelled bad and ached from their long journeys and the crowding. These were modest people, uncomfortable in the forced intimacy. Still, they were lucky and they knew it. Enforcement along the border was tougher than ever. Sheriffs in Phoenix were ignoring other crimes so they could catch people who came illegally from Mexico. Many friends had been caught and sent home. Others died in the desert. But they had come this far, alive and free.

Their journeys brought them from all over Mexico to Nogales. They sneaked across the border east of town, led by the *coyotes*, cutting through simple barbed wire that began where the tall iron fence ended. Then two new guides took over. They traveled almost two hundred miles from there, all six illegal immigrants in the back of an old van that rode low and wobbly, practically screaming at the Border Patrol to stop them.

But no *migra* showed that night. *Milagro, no la migra*, they joked, a little play on words to celebrate the miracle of escaping capture. Arizona State Patrol cars just rolled on by them in the desert darkness. The solo troopers inside seemed oblivious to a rickety van driving carefully under the speed limit. No traffic stops. No immigration checkpoints this night on the fast interstate highways. No delays all the way to Phoenix.

In the morning, one of the *coyotes* brought bags of food. There was a greasy breakfast sandwich for each person, cups of coffee for the adults, and a little carton of milk for the child. The small helping of cheap food tasted like a banquet. They had not eaten since yesterday afternoon. It was well known that many people coming north like this got nothing to eat for the entire journey.

No one gave them progress reports. They had paid in advance for passage to California. The van driver warned them that a day or two in Phoenix might be necessary while the drivers sized up enforcement on the roads. That was all they were told. So they waited.

At midday, they heard voices somewhere in the house. Then came footsteps. The door opened. Two *coyotes* stood there, flanking a short, muscular man. The travelers had not seen him before, but they knew instantly that he was *el jefe*. The boss. He did not smile. He showed no expression at all. He wore a shirt with images of tropical plants and parrots on it, and sharply pressed khaki slacks, and brown loafers so highly polished that they reflected the one weak light on the ceiling. Chicano, Pablo thought. Mexican ancestry, but an American. An American with money. Pablo sold fake Rolexes in Nogales for a while. He recognized the gold watch on this man's wrist as the real thing.

The boss looked at Pablo for only a moment. His attention moved quickly to Lourdes and her child. He nodded slightly, and Lourdes feared that she may have been singled out for grief. Her child or her pregnancy, perhaps, made her too much trouble.

The two young men stood in a corner near Pablo. The man's gaze did not even settle on them. The young woman had backed into the other far corner, as if pinned there by the gaze of the man in the doorway. She was tall, dark skinned, with the mature face and figure that come early to some Mexican girls. On the ride north, she had sat with Lourdes and played with Irma, but said little. The *coyotes* had noticed her, laughed and made half-hearted passes, but she had batted them away and nothing happened.

The boss raised his hand to beckon her.

"*Vente*," he said, using the familiar verb form, as bosses do, in a soft voice that was a command. It was a Mexican accent, Pablo guessed from the one word. This American had learned his Spanish along the border, somewhere from San Diego to Brownsville.

No one moved. Every one of the travelers looked at the young woman. Her name was Dulce. She came from a town near Hermosillo. They knew nothing else about her.

"*Ahora*," the man said. Now. "*Vente conmigo*." Come with me. The voice was still quiet, but more demanding.

Dulce stood a little taller, proud, but having no doubt that she would walk through the door or be dragged. She looked straight ahead and strode past the *jefe* without acknowledging him. The man turned to follow her. The *coyotes* closed and locked the door.

The footsteps faded and the house fell quiet. In the tiny room, Pablo went to Lourdes and held her. Their child slept on. The other two men stared at the floor, helpless and ashamed.

Somewhere in the building, a woman shouted angrily. Then they heard nothing from her. The house was silent again.

It was perhaps ten minutes until they heard sharp popping sounds outside. Many, in rapid succession. They came so quickly that no one could be sure if the sounds were shots or something else. They could hear men running, muffled shouting, sounds of confusion. Then, after minutes that felt like hours, footsteps came toward their door. The lock clicked and the door opened. The *jefe* was nowhere to be seen. But two new men stood there, one with a pistol, the other raising a shotgun.

2

Brinker

Some headline writer called it Immigration's Endless Summer. We thought it felt like most summers in Tucson. Too long, too hot, too many dead.

"I heard the coroner has ninety bodies in the morgue," I said.

"More by now," Al Avila said. He ran smoothly, breathed easily, and spoke as though he were standing still. "Almost all from the border. He had to rent refrigerated trailers for the overflow."

Al and I moved up our Saturday run to six a.m. The sun had barely risen and already blistered our backs. Al's neighbors would awaken soon, feel the heat, and wonder if they could gun the SUV to San Diego by lunchtime.

"That's just Pima County," I said. "It'll get worse. They can't keep up with the autopsies."

Thousands of people risked the illegal border crossing that year, hoping to make the Promised Land before the rumored new fences went up. The great recession had not yet pushed the economy close to collapse, so even newcomers without papers could find jobs. That year, the national angertainment industry discovered our long-running southwestern debate. Commentators raved. Politicians postured. No matter which side you took, somebody said you hate America. All the talk soon turned to white noise. The desert dust settled and the problems were still there.

The president flew in for photo ops. He ate Mexican food in Tucson and proclaimed Mi Nidito's chile relleno to be excellent. On the illegal immigration controversies, he promised something for everybody. Nobody was happy.

The National Guard built observation posts along the border. New recruits beefed up the Border Patrol. Self-styled civilian watchdogs reported for duty with lawn chairs, binoculars, and beer.

Still the people poured across. Many got through. Many got caught. Hundreds would die beneath a desert sun that punished us all that summer.

For me, born in the USA, Anglo, and not very political, life went on. So I thought, anyway, as Al and I ran on a cloudless mid-July morning. The blocks in his subdivision were five-hundred feet long, two-thousand feet around a square block. We figured that three times around made a little more than a mile. I was sweating and my hip still ached where a bullet hit it years earlier. Al glided along and seemed to gain energy with every block. He was a captain now, a senior desk job, but he kept the physique of a twenty-two-year-old patrolman.

"The whole immigration thing," he said. "God, aren't you glad we're out of that?"

Al and I had been Border Patrol agents together.

"We're never completely out of it, living here," I said.

"That reminds me," Al said. "You remember Carla Baca?"

It took a moment, but then I remembered Carla very well.

"Sure," I said. "I had some great teenage fantasies about her." I was breathing better and the hip pain eased as we slowed to a walk. "Unfulfilled, though. She didn't want to settle for any of us local yokels from Tucson High."

"Dreams of her own," Al said. "She went back east to Harvard."

"Everybody said she got straight A's."

"She's a big time immigration lawyer in L.A. now."

Yes, I remembered the striking girl from New Mexico who showed up one day in my sophomore English class. When Carla glided down the hall, long black hair gleaming, dark eyes looking straight ahead, you could almost hear the boys' knees buckling. Nobody had any illusions. Even the student body president and the quarterback didn't have a chance, let alone guys like us. Guys the vice principal called the Future Car Wash Employees of America Club.

"One of my regrets from high school," I said. "I never had the guts to say hello, let alone ask her out."

"I was in love with Anna already," Al said. "Got to admit, though, Carla got my attention whenever she walked by."

We reached Al's front door. I smelled fresh coffee and Anna's *sopaipillas*, just out of the pan.

"C'mon in," Al said. "If I'm left alone, I'll eat them all. Then I'll have to run another mile."

We headed for the kitchen. I said, "We're older and wiser now. We can understand that Carla was probably pining away, wanting us to call."

Al said, "That's what I meant to tell you. She called me yesterday. The poor thing has suffered long enough. She wants to see you. She said, 'Send Brinker over here.'"

"What?" I stopped at the kitchen door, waiting for a punch line.

"It gets better," Al said. "She wants to pay you."

I called Gabriela Corona to tell her that I would be in Los Angeles on Monday.

"Perfect timing," she said. "I just got back from Mexico."

"Doing a border story?" I asked.

"It's unbelievable," she said. "They have airlines for illegal immigrants."

"You're kidding."

"Swear to God," she said. "They fly from Mexico City to Mexicali or Hermosillo for a hundred dollars. They have vans at the airport to take passengers right to the *coyotes'* pickup points. It costs the same as the bus. It takes three hours instead of three days. You know what they call the airlines? *Aeromigrante*."

"That's a new one on me," I said.   "Anyway, I'll see you at dinnertime Monday."

"You're buying," she said.

"Sure," I said.   "In fact, I'll probably have a wealthy new client, so you can pick someplace expensive and decadent."

"Expensive and decadent," she said.   "Much like myself.   I'll make a reservation.   *Hasta luego*, sweetie."

3

Our Lady

From the air, the Los Angeles metro area appeared to creep farther east each time I made the flight. We came in over Palm Springs, more than a hundred miles out of L.A. To the west, a little empty land remained, but soon the solid tracts of housing and business began, their clutter unbroken to the sea. Visibility was limited, as usual, by some combination of smog and morning haze. Smoke, too. The pilot pointed out a cluster of stubborn brush fires in La Habra Heights. Several homes had already burned, he told us. More were threatened. He said we were twenty-two miles from LAX.

I was off the plane and into my rental car by eight-forty-five. It took until ten a.m. to slog through traffic. Carla Baca's office was on South Hope, about a block from the eastern end of Wilshire Boulevard. Wilshire ran from downtown toward the wealthy western precincts of L.A., through Beverly Hills, on to the ocean at Santa Monica. Not everyone got that far. Signs pointed to Immigration Court around the corner. I wondered how many people hauled in there ever made it west of Alvarado Street or the Rampart Division police station.

The Baca clientele seemed already assimilated and upwardly mobile. No huddled masses in the quiet waiting room. No anxious glances for *la migra* whenever the door opened. I gave my name to the receptionist and took a soft leather chair between an Asian man and a Latina with a very new baby in her arms. Both clients wore nice clothes and had good haircuts. They looked calm and confident. The man pored over his laptop computer, working on a spreadsheet. He probably had a green card in his pocket and a black Porsche downstairs. The woman rocked her baby softly and smiled as she admired the photographs on the wall.

The pictures advertised Carla. Several showed her with an arm around people of various races and ages. They held certificates of citizenship and small American flags. Robed judges smiled in a few photographs, shaking hands with newly sworn citizens. In another picture, a handsome young Hispanic couple held up their green cards as Carla beamed by their side. There was Carla in a three-shot with two older women in power suits. I recognized them as California's U.S. Senators. And there was the former President himself, shaking Carla's hand, doing his family values best not to look down her dress.

The door to the inner offices opened. A young, very tall man in a black silk suit and a dark blue turban said quietly, "Mr. Brinker?" I stood up and the man said, "Carla will see you now." He spoke with that elegant, deferential lilt that you hear in educated English speakers from India and Pakistan. He held the door as I walked through. The Asian and the Latina showed no surprise about my arriving last and getting in first.

Carla Baca stood at the end of the hall at her open door. The light from her office window framed her silhouette. My eyes adjusted and I recognized the face that could have been a prom queen's, if she had cared about that stuff.

"Brinker," she said. "Why, you're still a handsome boy. Just like I remember you." I found it odd that she remembered me at all, but her eyes twinkled and it didn't matter. I realized that in three years at Tucson High, I had seldom heard her speak.

"Now she tells me," I said.

Carla laughed. Her smile grew and the hallway warmed. Without a doubt, I was the most amusing guy in Los Angeles. She took my hand in both of hers, making it a firm handshake and a gentle pull into the office. I had recalled her being tall, but up close in high heels, she barely reached my shoulders. The long black hair was shorter now, turned stylishly at her neck, feminine and professional looking.

"Coffee?" she asked.

"Yes," I said. "Black, please."

She nodded at the man in the turban. He withdrew, pulling the door closed silently behind him. Carla led me to a sofa in a conversation area set away from her desk. The coffee table was made from the trunk of a giant redwood. It was cut to a smooth tabletop and polished to a hard gloss. We had a view west seventeen stories up.

"Nice," I said.

"Thank you," she said. "It took a while, but it is very nice. I help people become Americans and get paid well for it."

"How come you called Al?" I said. "I'm in the book. White and yellow pages."

"I knew he's a big shot on the Tucson P.D.," she said. "So I just asked my secretary to call him there. I never looked in the book."

"But here I am."

Carla smiled. "Here you are. I suspected that Al could tell me where to find you. This way, I get to talk with both of you. But it's you that I need."

"Be still, my heart," I said.

That laugh again. "Those needs are taken care of," she said. Cute but emphatic, friendly but no bull. "I mean a professional matter. I need your investigative magic."

"I don't have a license in California," I said. "No private eyes in Los Angeles?"

"Hundreds," she said. "But the good ones are all working for Hollywood people. Some of them used to, but they're in jail. Al said you're better than, how did he put it? 'A bunch of L.A. phonies,' I think. Besides, I need some work done in Arizona as well as California."

Carla stood and walked to her desk. I studied her walk carefully. She came back with a manila file folder.

"If you're available for a few weeks of work, I'd like to engage you officially right now. That way, my duty of confidentiality will attach to you as my employee. I have a simple contract and a retainer check here."

She passed the folder to me. Inside was a one-paragraph letter in which I agreed to provide investigative services for The Law Offices of Carla Baca and to maintain client confidentiality. Carla had signed it. There was space for my signature. The check was made out to me for ten-thousand dollars.

"Big job?" I said.

"I need you to sign before we discuss the matters to be investigated," she said. "Never fear. I wouldn't ask you to do anything illegal. Even if I did, you wouldn't have to. You know that."

I held up the check and said, "Non-refundable?"

"As long as you take the work," she said.

Where the letter of agreement said, "acknowledges receipt of the sum of ten-thousand dollars ($10,000.00)," I wrote in, "not refundable" and my initials. I had no idea if that carried legal weight, but it reassured me. I signed and passed the folder back to her. I kept the check.

"Anybody ever turn you down?" I said.

"It happens," she said. "I use O'Laughlin Security Services. They do security sweeps here and occasional protection if I'm involved in highly visible matters. They run investigations, too. The owner, Terry O'Laughlin, refused to pursue these issues."

She smiled and initialed my little amendment. She said, "I'll have a copy made before you leave."

She sat back and smiled like the Carla of my impossible adolescent dream. She had gained no weight that I could see. She still radiated that tingle, but the face had some lines and shadows never imagined in a high school princess's mirror. If I weren't seeing Gabi later, Carla might have crossed my mind as she had Al's.

"So, *mi jefa*," I said. "What's going on?"

She said, "Somebody is killing my clients."

4

The man in the turban returned with two big mugs of coffee in a brown and blue design that I recognized from Guadalajara. No fancy china or delicate biscuits. He placed them on the giant redwood and withdrew without a word.

"How many?" I said.

"I've had three incidents," Carla said. A strange way to describe killed clients, but I let it ride. She said, "Three in just two months."

"Too much for coincidence," I said. "The cops should be interested in that."

"If only," she said. "That's why I need you."

"What about your security firm? O'Laughlin, was it?"

"Terry O'Laughlin looked at the police reports and said these are going to be unsolved murders. Hopeless, he said. No clues going anywhere."

"What's wrong with the cops?" I asked.

"It's complicated," she said. "More than one agency is involved. We're talking about three different police departments in two states. Each department sees just one case, not three related cases. And they're not that good at talking to each other."

"Two states," I said. "Where?"

"Two cases here," Carla said. "The third is a little trickier."

"Trickier? The one in Arizona?"

"Yes, Arizona," she said. "But I want you to start here. The first time, it was right here in Los Angeles. Could you get to that right away?"

"I brought my toothbrush," I said. "I need to go home for a couple of days on Thursday, but I can come back next week and stay as long as necessary."

"I'll cover your hotels, of course," she said. "The Biltmore is right around the corner, if you want to be close. Meals, mileage, all that. Save your receipts."

"I'm thrifty," I said. "I won't need a hotel."

Carla smiled. "Miss Corona, I hear. She's a good reporter. She's been fair in the paper on immigration issues. I assume that she'll respect the confidentiality of your work."

"Tell me about the deaths," I said.

She stood again and returned to her desk. She sat down behind it, all business now, and opened another manila file.

"The first was José Liebowitz," she said. "Joseph, really, but he thought using José would help him with Mexican clients. He was a natural born U.S. citizen. His father was Mexican, came to this country legally, married an American woman. The father had a business supplying cameras and lenses to the movie studios, so José was always around the entertainment world. That led him into agenting. As the Latino population grew, he saw the market for international talent. He figured he was a natural because of his Mexican father."

"You helped him with the visas for his clients who were coming here to perform?" I said.

"To perform or to live here," she said. "We have so many Spanish speakers living in the southwestern states now. It's worthwhile for some of these entertainers to have a home base in this country. Most of them can't afford private jets, so they choose places with good air service and freeways, like Dallas or Phoenix or right here. That gives them easy access to all the Latino entertainment markets."

"Was Liebowitz having trouble with anybody?" I asked. "Any threats, vandalism at his office or home?"

Carla shook her head. "Nothing serious or specific that I know about," she said. "José mentioned that occasionally people would hear about his acts and make some racist or anti-immigrant crack, but he didn't say who the people were. And he didn't seem concerned."

"So what happened to him?"

"He was shot dead in his apartment one night. I'll show you the police report, but it's pretty thin. Nobody saw a thing. Nobody heard the shot."

"In an apartment building?"

"I know," Carla said. "I wondered the same thing. But it was a Friday night, and many of the tenants are young with some money. The building is near the Sunset Strip. It's not far to Beverly Hills or Westwood. Everybody was out partying."

"Security cameras?"

"Not that fancy a building. It's a perfectly nice place, but no doorman or high tech security. They do have a front door camera and monitors in the apartment so tenants can see who wants to come up. They don't record the camera, though. Visitors need to be buzzed in. That's it."

"What do the cops think?" I asked.

"Their investigation is continuing," she said in a tone that meant they had nothing.

"I'll have to talk with them," I said.

"I know. Good luck. I tried everything from flirting to obnoxious lawyer bluster. It's a dry well."

She found another file folder on her desk.

"Police reports on both cases," she said. "Not much there, but it might give you something to start with."

"Good."

"I'd like you to talk to José's sister at some point," Carla said. "Her name is Sandra Brown. She lives out in Riverside. She doesn't think enough is being done on José's murder. And she may know something about him that would be helpful."

"Okay," I said. "Tell me about the other one."

"Bo Bergstrom," she said. I thought she spoke his name with more sadness than José's. "Bo and his family have had a berry farm up at Camarillo for years. Whenever he came down here to see me, he'd bring a big jar of preserves or a box of fresh berries." She smiled at the memory.

"So you must have helped him with farm worker issues?"

"Exactly. Bo was very much opposed to illegal immigration. It's a pretty sensitive issue up there. Well, everywhere. So many of the farm workers are Hispanic. Some are legal, some not. Bo insisted that everybody have proper documentation of citizenship or legal residence. I made sure all the papers were legitimate. I got agriculture visas. I especially helped with non-citizens' work permits and tax matters."

"You think the murder had anything to do with his work?"

"The police haven't figured it out. It's hard to imagine Bo with any enemies. He was kind of a community leader up there. Gave lots to charities, that sort of thing. Just a wonderful man."

Her voice seemed to catch ever so slightly on the last words. I wondered if her relationship with Bergstrom was more than lawyer-client.

"Workers?" I said. "Business rivals?"

Carla shook her head. "He paid his workers more than other farms do. They had virtually no labor troubles. Nobody suspects a disgruntled employee. Some of the other growers may not have liked his way of doing business, but the idea of berry farm owners killing each other is just too bizarre to take seriously."

I opened the folder and glanced at the police report on Bergstrom.

"In his office," I said.

"Yes," Carla said.

"Did he keep money around?"

"It's not a cash business," she said. "They don't even have a berry stand out on the road, like some growers. He had a couple of hundred dollars in his pocket, so it wasn't robbery."

I took another sip of coffee. It was lukewarm now, but strong and good. I wanted another cup.

"I'll go up there tomorrow," I said.

"Let me have a friend of mine call you," Carla said. "His name is Richard Rawlins. He's an attorney here in town. He has a ranch up by Camarillo. He can help you with logistics, getting around, things like that."

"I can manage," I said.

"Rich will call you," she said.

"Have you pitched some kind of federal conspiracy angle to the feds?"

"The Arizona problem just happened," she said, "so there's no evidence of interstate crime yet. I thought about a conspiracy to interfere with lawful representation of immigrants, but that's a stretch. Anyway, my friend at the FBI just laughs. He says, 'Carla, we can't jump into conspiracy mode every time someone has a hunch. If we could cook up a homeland security angle, then fine. I could choose some suspects at random, take them to Egypt and torture them.' He's kidding, I hope. But he says forget federal involvement on this for now."

The man in the turban must have read my mind. He came into the room with a fresh pot of coffee, poured for Carla and me, and left without a word.

"Quiet fellow," I said.

"You would be, too, if you worked full time and went to law school at night. He has three kids at home," Carla said. "Some of us had it so easy. I probably got double minority points at school just for being a female Hispanic. I don't think Amric gets anything for being a Sikh man."

"He got into law school," I said.

"USC, with a scholarship on merit," she said. "And he'll get a place in this firm the day he passes the bar. Pure ability. He's smart and tireless and he really does want to help people."

We let that thought hang there to fill a silence. We looked out the big window and sipped our coffee.

"Colombian," she said, raising her cup. "Not by way of General Mills, either. This is straight from Bogotá. One of my clients brought it in yesterday. He said the customs guys gave it a hard look. The poor Colombians always get hassled. The drug dog took one little sniff and walked away, though.

"Good dog," I said.

"For a change," she said. "That dog and I are going to be fighting in court on a couple of cases."

"Bad dog," I said.

"My argument exactly, but it's not much," Carla said. "They'll bring him into court wearing his little doggie bulletproof vest. He'll sit there wagging his tail, grinning at the jurors with his tongue handing out. Hard to beat. I keep hoping for a jury full of cat people." She put down her coffee cup, sat back, took a breath, and exhaled slowly.

"Do you have any security for yourself?" I asked.

"I try to be careful," she said. "If I'm out in big crowds, or we get any threats, I use Terry O'Laughlin's tough boys."

"You've had threats?"

"Some of the anti-immigration people get crazy," she said. "Most places I go, it's a civilized discussion. But you never know when some wacko is going to throw taco sauce or dog poop."

"That ever happen to you?" I said.

"Not yet," Carla said. "It helps to have a couple of O'Laughlin's guys right next to me. They look like they played tackle in the NFL." She sneaked a peek at her wristwatch.

"What about the Arizona problem?" I asked.

"I'm still learning what happened over there," she said with an out-of-character dismissive snap in her voice. "Do these others first."

I rode the elevator down with a ten-thousand dollar check and a bunch of questions.

Why drag me over from Tucson when she had hundreds of investigators right in her own city? She could hire a one-man show like me or a whole agency. They weren't all in jail, no matter what she said. I had several good California-licensed investigators who helped me out when I needed extra eyes in L.A. I returned the favor in Tucson and we cheerfully billed each other's clients.

Why was she so worried about confidentiality when no live clients seemed to be involved? Why pretend to remember me when she barely knew me in high school?

My bank had a branch just down the block on Hope. I ducked in and deposited the check to my Tucson account. Before Carla changes her mind, I thought. Or before I change mine.

5

O'Laughlin Security Services kept a low profile at the back of a small office complex on Beverly Boulevard, near Wilton. The Paramount movie studios were on Melrose, just a few minutes north. O'Laughlin's front door bore a small logo with OSS in bold black type and a subdued gray L between the O and the first S. There was no company name, no hours of business, no phone number, no snarling guard dog image. A tiny camera lens peeked from above the doorframe. I pressed the button on a speaker box and gave my name. Carla had called to let them know that I was coming. Someone buzzed me in.

The outer office reminded me of an airlock. It had no receptionist. No windows. Two doors. It was just big enough for two matching wooden chairs in fake mahogany stain with black Naugahyde seat cushions. They showed no sign of ever having been sat in. I was about to try one when the interior door opened and a guy with a buzz cut stepped out, extending his hand.

"I'm Terry O'Laughlin," he said in a crisp voice, sharp but not unfriendly. He wore black slacks and a gray Tommy Bahama shirt painted with fronds from some unspecified tropic. The shirt hung straight down over a flat belly. He had forearms like Popeye and shoulders that barely made it through the door. I made him for forty-five but perhaps older than he looked. A career MP, maybe, who took the pension and put his cop skills to work in private industry.

He led me through another office where a young pretty woman was on the phone. She smiled as we passed. O'Laughlin punched numbers into a keypad on the wall. A door popped open and he held it for me. The guy apparently locked his own office door whenever he left the room.

"Paris Hilton must feel safe when she comes here," I said.

He laughed the way a sergeant laughs at a colonel's wisecracks. Hearty, but not too convincing.

"I don't do celebretards," he said. "I have a bunch of real stars, but they don't come here. I go to them."

"Ah, fame," I said.

"Fame. Big deal," he said. "Do this work for a while and you'd agree. Stars are like the rest of us, but they're dumb as dirt, most of 'em. Have a seat."

The guest chair was a duplicate of the reception room's. O'Laughlin had a big leather swivel behind a plain grey metal desk. He had a phone and a computer. There was one picture on the wall. It showed O'Laughlin and two other soldiers in desert camouflage with sergeant stripes. General Norman Schwarzkopf faced them, returning their salutes.

"You replacing me in Carla's affections?" he said, smiling at the absurdity of it.

"Not likely," I said. "What did she tell you?"

"That you're going to look into the departures of her two late clients," he said. "Lots of luck with that, pal. I've talked to the cops. They even let me see the files. Dead ends, both of 'em. I told her, forget it, babe. Carla, she thinks she's been around, but she has no clue. Her idea of violent crime is some drunk Mexican getting beat up on a traffic stop. She can no more think through a murder than she can clean an M-24."

A sniper rifle. Don't irritate this guy, I thought.

"She's hot, though," he said.

"I went to high school with her," I said. "That's pretty much a longstanding unanimous opinion."

"You score?" he said.

I tried to remember the last time some guy had asked me that. I just shook my head.

"Didn't think so," O'Laughlin said. "We shoulda gone to Hah-vuhd, you and me. Maybe we'd have had a chance."

"So what's your take on José Liebowitz and Bo Bergstrom?" I said.

He sat back in his chair and sighed. The chair squeaked as it reclined.

"Look," he said. "Carla thinks it's a big deal when a guy gets shot in his apartment. She can't understand what L.A. is really like. It's a rare day when some poor slob *doesn't* get shot in this town. And she's looking for a dark, exotic motive. She can't believe that people get murdered for no reason by psychos. But usually the reason is sex, drugs, or money. That's it. Sometimes in L.A. we hit the trifecta, you know, all three together. But there are no other motives."

"So," I said, "how does that play in these cases?"

He spread his hands. "Liebowitz, the guy up by Sunset, that looks like your basic Hollywood consumer transaction gone to shit. A hooker or a dealer, ten to one. They fight about the drugs or the sex, or the money to pay. Somebody pulls a gun and it's adiós, José. And you are never, ever gonna find that person unless he brags and some mope who needs a favor from the cops gives him up."

"Maybe," I said. "What about Bergstrom? The guy was a farmer, not some showbiz type on the Strip. You wouldn't tie him with sex and drugs."

O'Laughlin laughed. "What is it with you people? Farmers don't have sex and do drugs? Maybe in Kansas, but out here they can be snorting coke and diddling Toto, too."

"Carla doesn't think he was into anything like that."

"Oh, boy," he said. "She told you that?"

"Yes."

"Well, look," he said, "I don't know. Whatever. A guy wrote a book one time. He said the only thing you need to know about Hollywood is that nobody knows anything. Everybody thinks they do because they're smarter than the rest of us. Carla's like that. She's a minority woman and a lawyer. Well, actually, she'll be a majority if our demographics keep going like they are. You and me, we'll be the minority. Anyway, she thinks she's had the schooling and the real life education to understand human nature. But she doesn't know anything. This town lives on ignorance and high hopes of guessing right. Take those away, we're all on food stamps."

"So what's your guess on the murders?" I said.

"Liebowitz, like I said, drug dealer or hooker. Pretty classic scene, really. Bergstrom, who knows? Bad luck, maybe. He walks in his office, finds one of those Mexican berry pickers looking for the safe. Pedro pops him. No Bo, no mo'."

"You've been to Boot Hill in Tombstone," I said.

"Wyatt Earp," he said. "Get the bad guys in a corral and blow their sorry asses away. Those were the days."

I stood up. O'Laughlin sat there, looking up at me.

"Carla said you sweep her office. Find anything?"

"Nah. She's paranoid, but that's not a bad thing, actually. Checking her place is worth doing. But we never found any recording or transmitting devices or computer intrusions."

"What do you think about the coincidence?" I said. "Two of Carla's clients murdered in such a short time?"

"Shit happens," he said. "That's the best I can do. Nobody knows anything. That includes me."

"Thanks for the information," I said.

"And you're about to join the club," he said. "A week from today, you'll know less than you think you know now. Welcome to L.A."

6

On the car radio, I found an oldies station that called itself K-Earth. The dimwit disc jockey screamed with phony excitement, but the music mix was good and commercials were few. Gabi always listens to oldies. I figured she'd have the station on when I reached her place in Marina del Rey. As I parked the car, the station had just started playing Richie Valens.

Gabi answered the door wearing an oversized white terrycloth robe. The hem touched the carpet. She held a big fluffy towel. Her black hair was damp, gleaming, with a light scent of something fresh and floral. Sure enough, I could hear "La Bamba" on her kitchen radio.

"Hi, sailor," she said.

"*Yo no soy marinero*," I said. "*Soy capitán.*" Lyrics straight from Richie's song: I'm not a sailor. I'm the captain.

Gabi frowned. "Does that mean that I have to follow all your orders?"

"Strictly," I said. "But you can assume command later."

She gave me a radiant dirty smile and said, "Welcome aboard."

Later, Gabi said, "We could drive into Beverly Hills or Santa Monica for dinner. Or we could just walk around the marina to Café del Rey. That way we could drink all the wine we want and not worry about driving home. It's not too expensive or decadent, though."

"I can live with not too expensive," I said. "I think we took care of decadent already."

So off we went, arm in arm, old friends, lately something much better. I felt happy and lucky. Gabi laughed and teased and found adversity amusing. A case of mine once got her face smashed and her wrist broken. When I saw her injuries, she was cracking jokes about them.

Café del Rey was a bright place with earth toned walls, polished wood chairs, and a killer view of the marina. Diners scanned the room, chatting cheerfully, wondering who owned which boat. The menu was long on fish with Cal-Asian treatments. It had a couple of steak choices in case the former governor or some other large carnivore wandered in.

"So, Brinker," she said. "You want a key?"

"Love one," I said.

"My," she said, "that was easy." She took an apartment key from her purse and passed it across to me.

"I'll get a chain," I said, "and wear it close to my heart."

"I don't care where you wear it," she said. "Just keep it handy. Come back often and use it."

Gabi had chosen a champagne when we sat down. The bottle arrived and the waiter made a big show of popping the cork softly, without firing it into a passerby. He poured. Gabi smiled her approval. The waiter filled both our glasses and Gabi gave him an order for hors d'oeuvre.

"What do you know about Carla Baca?" I asked Gabi.

"Our lady," she said.

"Meaning?"

"She's the big local star in the immigration world," Gabi said. "Lots of clients, she's telegenic as hell, and she whipped the INS in court a few times. A magazine in Mexico City did an article on her. They called her *nuestra señora del norte*."

"Our Lady of the North," I said.

"I doubt if any normal human being calls her that," Gabi said, "but some Mexican editor did. A man from Sinaloa said Carla was a miracle worker for getting him a green card. A miracle from Our Lady."

"What's her reputation here?"

"Very good lawyer. Big publicity whore."

"You have those in L.A.?" I said.

Gabi laughed. "Oh, yeah. Carla craves coverage. She gets lots of it because she's gorgeous and feisty on immigration. That's about the hottest button you can push these days, so Carla's in demand."

The waiter came with a plate of Vietnamese duck spring rolls and an icy platter of oysters on the half shell with small cups of sauce and horseradish.

"Can't let your strength flag," Gabi said.

"You're always thinking of others," I said. She winked and speared a spring roll.

"So Carla's your wealthy client?"

"Right."

"What does she want you to do?"

I told her about José Liebowitz and Bo Bergstrom. "Have you heard of these cases?" I asked.

"José Liebowitz, yes," she said. "That wasn't my story, but it's hard to forget the name. The guy up in Camarillo, that rings a faint bell. I usually don't read the Ventura County section. But even Liebowitz didn't get much play here after the first couple of days. If you want your murders to have legs in the media, you have to kill several. Or one of the victims has to be a cute blonde girl."

"Well, what you just told me about Carla has me wondering," I said. "If she's so media hungry, how come she wasn't on TV, pounding the cops for more action on these killings? Call a news conference, say they're ignoring the obvious connection between two murders, blah blah blah."

"That would be her usual M.O.," Gabi said. "She's done that for less serious stuff."

"Something's going on," I said. "She's playing it close to the vest. She won't even tell me yet about part of her problem. Something in Arizona. I need to think about this."

Gabi forked an oyster off its shell, dipped it in the seafood sauce, and handed it to me.

"You need to think about that tomorrow," she said. "Tonight, you need to think about how wonderful it is over here. Lush life by the seaside. None of that hundred-and-ten degree Tucson craziness. Lots of interesting cases. Good money. Beautiful women. And when you get tired of beautiful women, there's always *moi*."

"You're beautiful," I said, and meant it.

"And skillful at extracting compliments," she said. "I'm lonely when you're gone, Brink. I have nice friends and a good job, but it isn't much fun when you're not here."

"Leaving Tucson would be tough," I said. "Maybe I'm like a saguaro. When it gets transplanted, it looks great for a while in the new location, then it dies."

"The big ones do," Gabi said, "but they're a hundred years old with ten arms. Young cacti can thrive in new ground. Especially if they get loving care."

"Maybe I'm young enough," I said. "I have only two arms."

"Just right for me," she said. "Brinker, those spring rolls and oysters were filling, don't you think?"

"We might not need an entrée," I said.

The waiter appeared, order pad in hand. Gabi said, "This was terrific, but I think we're going to head on home." She was grinning and her eyes sparkled and her hand was on my thigh.

"Straight to dessert, eh?" the waiter said. Gabi was still laughing after I paid the bill and she led me back across the marina.

7

My cell rang at seven o'clock. I was pouring orange juice and Gabi was making coffee in her little kitchen overlooking a row of boat docks.

"Mr. Brinker," the man on the line said, "I'm Richard Rawlins. Friend of Carla Baca."

"She mentioned you," I said.

Rawlins said, "Carla asked me to give you a fast ride up to Camarillo today." His voice had a touch of Texas. There was a little accent and a hint of swagger. No drawl. His speech was quick and clipped.

"It's only a couple of hours," I said. "I appreciate the offer, but I can drive myself."

"Are you kidding?" he said. "It'll take you two hours to get to Culver City this time of day. You're at the marina, right?"

"Right."

"Okay. Drive over to LAX. Go into the parking garage opposite American Airlines. I'll meet you on the roof."

"The roof?" I asked, starting to wonder about this guy.

"We're taking my helicopter," he said.

I said, "Now you're kidding."

"I'm a lawyer," Rawlins said. "Would I lie?"

He probably guessed right about the traffic. It took me forty minutes to go just six miles from Marina del Rey to LAX. I wondered how close Los Angeles was to perfect gridlock. One last car would squeeze onto some freeway and everything would stop. No more high-speed chases. Television stations would go bankrupt.

I drove to the top parking level and left the car near the Heliport stairs. A man leaned against the stairway door, holding it open. He was a short, compact guy with black hair, thinning on top, combed back. I made him for late fifties or maybe sixty. He dressed attorney casual, with grey slacks, a blue button down shirt open at the collar with no tie, and a leather pilot's jacket.

"Mr. Rawlins?" I said.

"Rich," he said, extending his hand. His shake was firm and his smile was easy. Just what you want in a lawyer or a pilot. "Good to meet you, Brinker. C'mon."

He led us up one level and onto the roof. The helicopter looked brand new. From twenty feet away, I could see our reflection in the metallic royal blue paint. The registration number, N187RR, was stenciled in gold on the tail boom. The main rotor perched on an inverted cone-shaped assembly that rose from just aft of mid-cabin.

"The RR stands for Richard Rawlins?" I asked.

"Too egotistical?" he said, laughing. "Hell, I don't care. You know what the 187 stands for?"

"Wanna bet?" I said.

"I never bet unless I know the outcome," he said. "And you know it, I figure."

"It's the California Penal Code section for murder," I said. "It's in Carla's reports on the cases here."

"Good for you," he said. "I used to practice family law, but there's more money in murder. Murder is one of Southern California's leading industries."

"It bought you a nice helicopter," I said.

"It helped. Robinson R-44," Rawlins said. "Brand new. Built just down the road in Torrance. I picked it up at the factory myself and flew it off the field. Had it only a couple of months."

"Maybe I'll drive after all," I said.

"Ha!" Rawlins slapped me on the back. "Never fear, my friend. I put more than five-thousand hours on my old ones. I have a commercial pilot certificate. And I flew choppers in the Navy, back in a previous life. Your survival chances are good."

He opened the left door and watched as I climbed up and settled in. The elaborate seat belt and chest harness had four clips. Rawlins helped me fit the rig, moving his hands quickly.

"How do you know Carla?" I asked.

"Met her at a continuing legal education program," he said, fiddling with the last buckle. "We have to go to those classes to keep our licenses. They're utterly useless crap. The bar association steals our money and pretends we're improving the profession. But that one was worth it. I saw her across the room and that did it."

"Zing went the strings of your heart?"

"Like the whole Charlie Daniels Band and the Houston Philharmonic put together," he said, laying on the Texas twang.

"You must have had to get in line," I said. "Guys have been falling in love with Carla since high school."

"Still the same," he said, laughing. "But she keeps them at a safe distance."

"You, too?"

"Whatever distance she wants," Rawlins said. "It's always Carla's call. Once you figure that out, you're fine."

He went around to the right side and climbed in. He handed me a pale green headset-microphone unit and put on his own. He flipped a few switches and waited about thirty seconds, then fired the starter. I could feel the rotor turn and gather RPM's.

"Hear me okay?" he said, his voice crackling through the headset.

"Loud and clear."

"Okay, good. It's voice activated. Just talk when you want to. But stay quiet when I'm talking to a controller."

"Right."

He listened to recorded airport information, then called the tower for takeoff clearance. As he spoke, a 767 lifted off to our right and a dinky regional jet was aloft to the left.

The controller came back, speaking in the staccato bursts of an auctioneer. "Robinson one-eight-seven Romeo Romeo, Los Angeles tower. Westbound departure and shoreline transition approved. Remain at or below 125 feet. Keep it between the runways, sir, and turn north at the coast. Clear for immediate takeoff."

Rawlins had the chopper in a hover when the controller said "immediate." The skids were maybe three feet off the rooftop. He pushed the nose down and the helicopter eased forward. We glided off the parking structure, picking up lots of speed and just a little altitude. We headed almost due west toward the ocean, passing over the international terminal. Rawlins kept the chopper right between the pairs of runways on the north and south sides of the airport. I heard the controller say, "Air New Zealand seven-four-four heavy, clear for takeoff, runway two-four left."

We reached the beach in less than two minutes. Rawlins banked to the north. "Look to your right," he said. A 747 was lumbering up, wheels retracting. The unmistakable shape seemed to head right for us, but it passed behind and far overhead.

"Nonstop to Auckland," Rawlins said. "Thirteen hours in the air. Amazing."

He asked LAX for permission to change radio frequencies. The controller approved. Rawlins moved a dial on the radio and called Santa Monica airport's tower. The controller there approved flight past the SMO traffic area at five-hundred feet above the coast.

"Look down there," Rawlins said. "Spot your honey, maybe."

We zipped past Marina del Rey. I looked for Gabi's apartment but couldn't place it as we hit a hundred knots and left the marina complex behind. A few early beach walkers waved as we approached a little amusement park jutting over the water.

"Santa Monica Pier," Rawlins said. The helicopter climbed up to eight-hundred feet. "Few minutes we'll be at Malibu. I'll give you a quick tour of the stars' homes."

The coastline bent westward as we neared Pacific Palisades. Cliffs rose east of the coast highway, forcing the expensive real estate away from the beach. It looked public down there, a vast expanse of sand with parking lots behind it. Automobiles on the highway stood still. I relished the freedom of soaring along with no traffic in our way.

Rawlins switched radio frequencies. He turned another knob and I heard country music playing softly in my headset.

"Sunset Boulevard coming up," Rawlins said. "Malibu five miles ahead."

"What do you think of Carla's clients turning up dead?" I said.

"Pretty damn strange," he said. "Hardly beyond the realm of random misfortune, though. Carla sometimes sees the world in conspiratorial terms."

"How do you mean?"

"Take the guy in West Hollywood. That could've been a burglary. Could have been a neighbor with a bad temper, or some crank skank who just wanted his money. I don't see what he had in common with the berry farmer besides Carla's being his lawyer. Carla mentioned that Bergstrom always worked late on Tuesday nights. Everybody at the farm probably knew that. If I were the cops, I'd be looking at employees."

"Did you know either one, Liebowitz or Bergstrom?"

"I think I met them once or twice at parties. I might have run into them at Carla's office. But I didn't know them."

"What did you mean when you said Carla sees the world in conspiratorial terms?"

"Oh, nothing, really," he said. "It's not uncommon. In law school, we called it 'thinking like a lawyer.' She puts one and one together and comes up with a plot."

"What does she say when you tell her that?"

"Tell her that?" Rawlins said. He laughed. "You have a few things to learn about Carla, my friend."

"How so?" I asked.

"This is a great helicopter," he said. "I'm a damn good pilot. But I won't fly into a thunderstorm."

"Carla have a temper?"

He smiled and said, "She can get a little turbulent."

We were off Malibu now. The tightly packed beach houses of the lower tier rich flashed by.

"That's Pepperdine University up there," Rawlins said. He pointed to a spread of modern construction on a steep slope rising inland from the highway. "I taught a few courses at the law school. My Lord, between the view and the girls, I don't know how anybody studies."

It looked like Ronald Reagan's shining city on a hill, come to life. A great sprawling campus, with sparkling new buildings on fields of year-round seaside green. It surely had more eye-popping panoramas than any movie star's house down below.

He eased the chopper's nose up. We slowed and gained altitude.

"We're getting to serious money now," he said. "That's Barbra Streisand's chateau on top of the cliff a few miles ahead. I try to give her some room when I fly by. She sued a guy who flew down the whole state, taking pictures of every foot of coastline. Said it invaded her privacy."

"She win?"

"Hell, no," he said. "It was a total non-starter. But you know how people are. They win a few Oscars, make a billion dollars, they think they're special."

He pointed out the oddly shaped house where Johnny Carson had lived, and Kenny G's place, and the Julia Roberts estate.

"Lot of the new stars live down there, but I don't know who the hell they are," he said. "I fly my little nieces around and they get all excited about finding some rapper's house. I say, look, Cher lives right over there on that flat, and they just roll their eyes."

"What happened in Arizona?" I said.

"You'll have to ask Carla about that," he said.

"Yeah, well," I said, "she's avoiding that subject. She hires me to look into it, but won't talk about it. I get a bad feeling here."

"So, quit and keep the advance," he said.

We had pushed past the Streisand castle and Point Dume. Rawlins turned north, flying above the brown brush of the Santa Monica Mountains.

"In the winter, all that would be green," he said. "In summer, it dries out. Turns into a tinderbox."

I said, "What do you think of O'Laughlin, the security guy?"

"OSS," Rawlins said. "Don't you love that? Like the old CIA. He has harmless delusions of grandeur. Thinks nobody can be safe without him. But he's okay at what he does. They sweep Carla's office for bugs, check the file cabinet locks and the computer security. If Carla's going somewhere with potential for problems, like a college talk or an immigration rally, he sends a few bruisers to escort her. O'Laughlin usually comes along himself. I think he has the hots for Carla. Anyway, he's good for routine security. I wouldn't hire him to solve any crimes of the century."

"Why does Carla need her office swept for bugs?" I said.

"She's in an adversarial business," he said. "One of her primary adversaries is the government. You think some agency wouldn't spy on her to see what's happening along the border? They don't need an excuse since 9/11. They just call it terrorism prevention and do whatever they want. She's lucky they haven't hassled her with some bullshit indictment. Even with O'Laughlin's snoops cleaning the place every week, I wouldn't do anything more confidential than order lunch on her phones or computers."

Soon we came over great rectangular patterns of farmland. I hadn't known there was any left this close to L.A.

Rawlins said, "We're in Ventura County now." He switched radio frequencies again and called the Camarillo airport. It was a single runway field with a big cluster of businesses on the south side. The controller cleared us to land to the west.

Rawlins rogered that. He said to me, "I have a little ranch up here. My manager brought a couple of vehicles down. You take one for your interview and I'll take the other one to the ranch. We'll meet at the airport later and I'll fly you back."

"What's your relationship with Carla, exactly?" I asked.

"Depends on the moment," he said. "Lawyer, pilot. Warm voice on the phone when the night gets cold."

"Sounds like a full time job."

"It can be," he said. "I'm available for whatever she wants me to be, whenever she wants it."

"Got it that bad, huh?" I said.

He smiled and turned his attention to the approach.

"I Got It Bad," he said. "That's a country song. Lot of wisdom in country music, Brinker."

We were still doing eighty knots as the field loomed close. I remembered the Border Patrol pilots hot-dogging for their fellow agents. I knew that Rawlins would do what they called a speed stop, sucking the airspeed rapidly down to zero and going into a hover right over the touchdown spot.

"Yep, that bad," he said, as much to himself as to me. He kept his eyes on the rising runway.

8

Two Asian men stood by a Range Rover painted metallic blue to match the helicopter. I wondered if Rawlins bought it, too, for the initials. Next to the Range Rover was an old Jeep Cherokee in mud-splattered gray. I was pretty sure of which one would be my ride.

One of the men gave me the Jeep keys and a paper with directions to Bo's Berries. He had known I was coming and where I was going. His hand-drawn map suggested taking Lewis Road.

"It's a little out of the way," he said, "a couple of miles or so. But you'll get a better look at the country. Lots of work going on out there. Not all legal like Bo's, either."

I headed east until Pleasant Valley Road met Lewis, then I turned south. Rawlins's man had left the air conditioning on. I switched it off and put down my window. The air was cool but the sun was high enough to warm it gently. A strong smell of onions hit me as I moved along Lewis Road.

Plastic sheet fences and windbreaking shrubs blocked my view of several fields. In others, I saw crews working steadily, bent over the crops. Men and women were dressed in layers of sweaters and jackets, readily changeable for the fickle coastal climate. Battered school vans and busses, their old yellow bodies and black safety markings painted over in grimy white, stood by the fields.

I almost missed the small sign pointing up a dirt road to Bo's Berries. The Cherokee bumped along for a half mile until I arrived at a well-kept clearing and a small ranch house. The sign over the front door said, "Office."

The place didn't look like the headquarters of a successful modern agriculture company. A gray-haired woman with a pleasant smile sat at a gray metal desk, turning over papers and pounding numbers into an old-fashioned adding machine. She had a desktop computer but it didn't seem to be turned on.

"Hi," she said. "I bet you're Mr. Brinker."

"Morning," I said. "I am."

"Well, come on in," she said. "Bill's expecting you."

She stood and led me into another room. A slender, tanned man with short fair hair sat behind another gray metal desk. There was a growers' co-op calender on the wall, next to a framed photograph of the first President Bush. I made out "To Bo" on the inscription. The man stood up and came around the desk to greet me.

"Bill Bergstrom," he said. He gave me a hearty farmer's handshake. "Thanks for coming up, Mr. Brinker." He pointed me to a straight back wooden chair and resumed his place behind the desk.

"I'm sorry about your brother," I said.

"Thank you," he said. "I appreciate your helping us."

"I won't kid you," I said. "There's not much chance of my discovering something the police haven't."

"I understand," Bergstrom said. "And I have no complaints about the investigation. Our family has been in business here for forty years. I've known the county sheriff since second grade. We played basketball together in high school. I don't make a big deal of it, but we do get our phone calls returned, if you know what I mean."

"Carla thinks there might be a connection with the murder of another client of hers," I said.

"It is strange," he said. "I'm positive that Bo didn't know Mr. Liebowitz. I sure didn't. Nobody else around here did, either. We've asked. Not just our family, but the employees, too. Nobody had heard of him before Carla told us what happened."

"Yes," I said. "You see what that suggests. If there's a connection, it's Carla herself. That's why she hired me. To find out about that."

"Right. She expressed that concern. Carla means a lot to all of us in the family and the company. For a while there, we thought that she and Bo might have, you know, a little romance. Probably wasn't in the cards, but she's a dear friend to us. She feels terrible that something about her might have caused this. I don't believe that for a minute, but I'd sure like to put her mind at ease."

"Well, if she is the connection," I said, "it must have something to do with her immigration work. That's what your brother and José Liebowitz had in common with her."

Bergstrom leaned back in his chair. It was an old wooden swivel chair. It creaked.

"A lot of people are riled up about immigration these days. Some have legitimate concerns. There are plenty of problems we need to deal with. Some other people are just xenophobes or tinfoil heads. You know, immigration is a Trilateral Commission U.N. one world plot."

"I was on the Border Patrol," I said. "I've met them all."

"The thing is," Bergstrom said, "it doesn't make sense that any of those people, good or bad, would hurt Bo. We were one of the leaders around here on checking legal status. We confirm employee identities. It cost a lot, but it's come back to us a thousand-fold in good community feelings, labor relations, everything. If there's ever an INS raid or some showoff election year crackdown, we're golden. And Bo was the driving force on that. Our dad, we called him Big Bo, he thought we were nuts at first. But he realized it was smart. So why Bo, of all people?"

I stood and looked out the small window. Berry patches in all directions to the limit of my vision. No onion smell here. A faint haze overlaid the fields and blurred the horizon, reminding me how close this farmland was to the ocean.

"If it wasn't some anti-immigration person," I said, "how about someone who profits from illegals?"

"You mean one of our competitors?" Bergstrom said.

"It occurred to me. We're grasping for motive here."

He shook his head. "It's not that kind of competition," he said. "We compete aggressively, sure, but no cutthroat stuff. We help each other. Borrow each other's equipment, work up common talking points on business issues. When we go see our legislators to get a little help, we go together. Agriculture is a big complex enterprise now, but when you strip everything away, we're just farmers. We're prudent people, in our business and our lives. I don't think there's a chance of what you're suggesting."

"Bo had no personal enemies?" I asked.

"If he did, I didn't know them," his brother said. "Or even know about them. He was friends with everybody."

"I understand that he often worked late on Tuesday nights."

Bergstrom smiled. "He liked the quiet. No distractions. He could spend a lot of daytime hours in the fields, and get the desk work done at night. No Monday nights because of football on TV."

"Lots of people know that he worked late on Tuesdays, alone?"

"I suppose. But those would have been his friends."

"An employee?" I asked. "Maybe he walked in and found someone rifling the office?"

"Deputies looked into that, first thing," Bergstrom said. "They found no evidence of a robbery attempt. And if it had been an employee, I'll tell you honestly, I think some other employee would have turned him in. We have great relationships with our people. We've worked hard at it. If I walked out in the fields right now, I'd know every person by name. So did Bo." He shook his head. "Nope. I'm just not buying an employee for this."

I gave him a business card and we shook hands.

"If you think of anything that might be helpful, call me or Carla," I said.

"I will," he said. "And you let me know if I can do anything for you. Our files, our employees, everything is at your disposal if you believe it could help. We can fax documents to you, scan them and email them, whatever you need."

I glanced at the computer on his desk. Like the machine in the outer office, it was off.

Bill Bergstrom smiled. "It works," he said, "but most of our real work is in those fields out there."

I drove back toward the airport. At a pullout on Lewis Road, a few miles from Bergstrom's property, I stopped and watched another farm's crew. It must have been break time. A bus was parked on the dirt entry road. Most of the crew walked toward it.

I got out of the Jeep to stretch my legs. Several Hispanic men saw me. They looked away, put their heads down, and walked more quickly to the bus. The same thing happened at job sites around Tucson. I had taken off the uniform years ago, but among some people, something about me still said *la migra*.

9

Richard Rawlins must have seen me coming. He had the R-44's rotors turning when I drove through the airport entrance. His man took the Jeep keys and I climbed into the helicopter. Rawlins checked my seat belt, said something to the air traffic controller, then we burrowed into the west wind and climbed. He swung the chopper into a smooth turn and headed southeast, toward the coastline.

I put on my headset. He said, "Crack the case?"

"Not yet," I said.

Rawlins laughed. When neither of us was speaking, I could hear the unmistakable twang of George Strait at low volume in the headset.

"I told Carla you wouldn't get much, even if you're as good as people say," he said. "She's dreaming, though. She figured you'd nose around a little, find the clue that four professional homicide cops with about sixty years experience missed."

"She's smarter than that," I said.

"She's smarter than anything, but it doesn't matter," he said. "Wishes trump facts. The heart overpowers the brain. You hear George there?" He leaned forward and turned up the music volume a little. "All my ex's live in Texas. Happens to describe me perfectly. My marriage history shows you the power of hope over experience. That's true whether Samuel Johnson says it or George Strait sings it."

"So you try to protect her from her heart?"

"I wouldn't put it that way," Rawlins said. "I inject a little harsh reality into her analysis sometimes. Just for balance."

"You want to marry her?" I said.

"Let me give you a helicopter lesson," he said. "Grip your left hand around that handle by your left leg there. That's called the collective. You want to go up, you pull that up gently. Down, you ease it down. Leave it where it is for now, but hold on to it."

He saw that I had the handle in my grasp. "Fine," he said. "Now put your right hand on that vertical handle of the T-bar in front of you. That's called the cyclic. We use it to turn and help adjust airspeed. Move it around a little. Real gently, now."

I pushed the cyclic to the right and the helicopter tilted and lurched that way. It felt as though we were rolling over. I pulled my hand away. Rawlins laughed as he eased us upright and back on course with only his fingertips on his set of the dual controls.

"That's the answer to your question," he said. "Go slow and easy. No hasty movements. Be gentle. Don't try to make her do something she's not designed for."

"Did I almost kill us?" I said.

He removed his hand from the cyclic and patted the instrument console. He said, "This sweetheart, she's very forgiving. Unlike some."

I got back to Gabi's apartment at two-thirty. She had left a note and a large manila envelope on the kitchen table. "Brought this back at lunchtime. Have you heard about it?" the note said.

She had printed out an Associated Press story dated the day before.

PHOENIX, Ariz. (AP) Four people were found shot to death in a house just west of Sky Harbor airport, Phoenix police Chief Herbert Kalven said.

Evidence at the scene indicated that all the victims were Mexican nationals, Kalven said. He said that the shootings took place sometime within the last week.

"The circumstances lead us to believe that these people were part of or victims of a smuggling ring," Kalven said.

Kalven said the murder house is on a largely abandoned block condemned by the city last year. The other houses are not presently occupied and were to be demolished next month to make way for a new retail complex. This would account for the absence of complaints despite the long time the bodies were in the building, Kalven said.

The police chief declined to answer questions, citing the early stage of the investigation.

A source close to the investigation said that other persons had been staying in the house where the bodies were found. The source spoke on condition of anonymity because only the police chief was authorized to make statements on the case.

At the bottom of the page, Gabi had written, "Carla's case?"

I thought of the ninety bodies in the Pima County morgue. The victims in Phoenix had evaded the killing heat of the desert border country. They probably thought they were home free. Then they were slaughtered in what they surely considered a safe house. It was an old story: illegal immigrants jammed into tiny quarters, awaiting the next leg of their journey. Usually, though, it ended when the Border Patrol found them, or when the *coyotes* simply abandoned them.

Shot within the last week, the chief thought. This was Tuesday. Carla had called Al on Friday. I have a low tolerance for coincidence. This really pushed it hard.

The reporter's byline said Thomas R. Jenkins. The story showed that Jenkins had a friend on the force. If this was Carla's Arizona case, I would be getting acquainted with Tom.

Gabi had attached another printout, apparently an update of the first story.

PHOENIX, Ariz. (AP) Police this afternoon said that other persons may have been in the Sky Harbor area house where four people were found shot to death.

"Evidence at the scene leads us to believe that at least two other people were present at some time with the victims," police Chief Herbert Kalven said.

Kalven told a crowded news conference at police headquarters that the evidence included clothing, personal items, and "some forms of identification." He declined to provide names of the missing persons.

A reporter asked whether police were attempting to contact relatives of the identified victims in Mexico.

Kalven, who speaks Spanish, said, "I will be making some of those calls myself."

Kalven was asked about widespread speculation that a gang paid to smuggle immigrants had killed them instead.

"We don't know yet what happened," he said. "Taking that question as a hypothetical, I would tell you that some smugglers do what they promise, but others will cut your throat in an instant. Whatever happened here, this should be a warning to others who try to enter illegally. You just can't be sure whether your guides are helpers or killers."

Asked again if he believed that the victims were slain by immigrant smugglers, Kalven said, "No conclusion is possible at this time, based on the evidence available to us."

Maybe, I thought. But I wondered how much more evidence was available. I wondered how much Carla Baca could tell us.

10

José Liebowitz had lived in unincorporated West Los Angeles, so his murder was a county sheriff's case. I called the station in West Hollywood and asked for Detective Cliff Jansson. His name was on the report Carla had given me.

"Why would I want to talk to you?" he said.

"To partner with the people you serve, seeking innovative ways to protect the public?" I said.

"Where'd you get that hogwash?"

"Off the sheriff's web site."

"Oh, brother," he said. "First I got Carla threatening to file civil rights suits on me every time I arrest a Mexican. Now she brings in visiting PI's to smartass me. I love my job."

"I'll buy you a beer," I said. "It's a time-honored investigatory technique of smartass private eyes."

"I quit drinking," he said. "Otherwise the doc said my liver was putting in for early retirement. You know where the Farmers Market is?"

"Sure," I said.

"Bennett's Ice Cream. It's inside the market, the old part, on the east patio. You can buy me a cone. Make it 4:30." He hung up.

Fourteen miles from the marina. I had about an hour and half to get there in afternoon rush hour traffic. I left immediately.

Jansson was easy to pick out. He was a sandy haired guy with a stretch-knit era jacket that would never again button over his gut. He stood back from the counter, reading the list of ice creams. He felt me coming, the way cops do, and turned around.

"Brinker?" he said. I said hello and we shook hands.

"I was thinking maybe a scoop of chocolate and a scoop of strawberry on a sugar cone," he said. "I don't like those weird flavors and funny names." I nodded and ordered his cone, plus a single of the orange sherbet for me.

"You don't look like a weight watcher," Jansson said.

"My sweetie is making dinner tonight," I said. "If I'm not hungry, there could be trouble."

"Let's take a walk," he said. "We start talking about exit wounds here at the counter, the customers get nervous."

We headed into the aisles of the old shopping center. It had been around since the 1930's. It really was a market for farmers back then. It still looked like one, but now the farmers came by the tourist busload from Kansas and Korea and all points in between. The landmark white wooden clock tower is dwarfed by glitzy modern stores nearby. Inside, though, walking from stall to stall, you still feel the old L.A.

"I like to come here every couple of weeks," Jansson said. "Go next door to the big new center, you can buy a suit for a thousand dollars, all kinds of expensive useless shit. Here it reminds me of being a kid, coming in for an ice cream or some taffy with my folks. Got any place like this in Tucson?"

"No," I said. "My favorite spot is a baseball diamond at the elementary school in my old neighborhood. My dad took me in there on weekends, taught me how to hit and field. I still go back there once in a while to watch the kids play."

"Don't try standing outside a school fence watching kids here," he said. "Pervert alert. We'd send the SWAT team after you. Shoot to kill."

I laughed. We turned the corner to another row of food stalls. They sold gleaming fish and plump vegetables.

"There used to be a great ball park right up the street," Jansson said. "Gilmore Field. The old Pacific Coast League played there before the Dodgers and Giants came out west. Tickets for a buck. Kids two bits. God, I'm old."

We passed a bakery offering fresh bread stacked high in a wicker basket. I took a deep breath and saw Jansson do the same. We laughed.

He said, "Carla thinks we're screwing it up."

I shrugged.

"We're stuck right now, maybe, but we're giving it all we got. And we haven't messed up anything. You ever a cop?"

"Border Patrol," I said.

"Oh, boy," he said. "When I'm having a lousy day, I tell myself, just thank God you're not on the Border Patrol."

"I know the feeling," I said.

"Anyway, you know the drill. We get the crime scene worked, the evidence collected. Hell, everybody with a TV knows this stuff now. We talk to all the neighbors, talk to next of kin, friends. We pull the guy's bank accounts and credit cards and try to find his favorite bartender and who he was sleeping with. We're okay on this, Brinker, no matter what your Ms. Baca thinks."

"She doesn't know what to think yet," I said.

"Oh, yeah?" Jansson said. "That would be a first."

"Somehow," I said, "I don't think you appreciate Carla."

"Actually, I do," he said. "It's always fun when she comes by, 'cause she's got a great little ass and she starts out being real sweet. Pretty soon she heats up, though. Says we're not trying hard because the victim was Hispanic. I say, 'Carla, the *sheriff's* name is Baca, for chrissakes.' She says, well then, it's because the victim was a Jew, too. I say, 'Carla, it's West L.A. We got more Jews than Tel Aviv. Steven Spielberg gets knocked off, we're gonna drag our feet?' Her mind's made up, though. Injustice runs amok. Carla Baca to the rescue."

We stopped at a stall called Light My Fire. It sold nothing but hot sauces. There seemed to be hundreds of them from around the world. Some were familiar salsas. Others had names like Rocket Fire and Toxic Waste.

"How do they make a living here?" Jansson said.

"Angelinos from everywhere," I said.

"Yeah, but how much of this stuff can people eat before their guts explode?"

"In Tucson, we put salsa in the baby formula," I said.

"So you guys are immune," he said. "You ever try any of this hot Korean stuff? Man, eat some of that, you can park your sinuses in a handicap spot."

I said, "What did you get from your investigation so far?"

"Carla didn't give you the reports?" he said.

"Yes, she did."

"She tell you I gave them to her, more than I had to, because I'm such a wonderful guy?"

"I don't recall her mentioning that," I said.

"Well, you know what I know about the late José. Quiet neighbor. No trouble. Sleepover girls now and then, but nobody regular. One shot to the back of the head, up close."

"That sound like an L.A. burglar?" I said.

"Nope," he said. "Looked like a pro to me. But we don't quite have anything connecting him to anybody like that. I don't think it was a burglar because the building is fairly secure. Not much history of problems. There's no doorman, but you need a key or a buzz-in from one of the apartments. Best bet is that José took somebody upstairs and that was a big mistake."

"Money?"

"Haven't really got into that yet. You know, Brinker, we had four-hundred-two murders last year in L.A. County. Just the county, not the city. I'm what you call a busy guy."

"You said 'not quite' anything to put him with bad guys. You know anything that's not in the report on Liebowitz?"

"Between you and me?"

"Okay," I said.

"We're getting a few hints that José might have done some drugs," he said. "That's not for sure, so don't get your hopes up."

"What kind of drugs?"

"Well, that's part of the problem," he said. "We don't know what kind. Pot, nobody really gives a shit except politicians having news conferences. I could walk up to some guy on the street corner, show him my shield, and he'd sell me some. But maybe it was something nastier."

"You haven't found a dealer?"

"Nope. Just neighbor talk so far. And for God's sake, don't tell Carla. She'll be down at my office, screaming about drug rumors to blame the victim."

We walked toward the exit to the parking lot.

"What do you think of Terry O'Laughlin?" I asked.

Jansson shrugged. "Good at what he does. He thinks he's James Bond. Brags about his surveillance equipment. It's better than what I can get. Likes to hint that he holds the secrets of the rich and famous, but if he tells you, he'd have to kill you. That kind of guy. Plays it legal, though, far as I know."

We stopped at a white Ford four-door sedan with three radio antennas.

"Undercover car," he said. "You know how we'll break this case, don't you?"

"A rat," I said.

"Bingo," he said. "A deputy'll see a broken window, pull in to check, and there's some asswipe carrying a flat screen TV out the back door. They'll be riding down to the lockup and the creep'll say, 'You know that dead guy up by Doheny and Sunset?'"

"And they'll give him a deal to finger Liebowitz's killer."

"Correctomundo," Jansson said. "Carla will find out it has nothing to do with immigration law or José being Mexican, and she'll come in hollering cover-up."

"I'm surprised you don't tell her to get lost," I said.

"I do," he said. "If I were nice to her, I'd escort her out to the lobby. Hold the door for her. Give her a nice west side air kiss and thank her so much for dropping by. But if I kick her out, I can sit behind her, watch that little butt wiggle out the door."

"Important to know your adversary," I said.

"From all angles," he said. "Keep it in mind. If you get onto something, somebody might get onto you. Thanks for the ice cream."

11

Gabi's Miata was in the carport. I hustled upstairs and used my key. She was in the kitchen, barefoot, wearing a bright green apron over black slacks and a white blouse. She was slicing tomatoes that looked even better than the ones at Farmers Market. Two steaks sat on the counter. Gabi turned on the broiler.

"I thought about wearing just the apron," she said.

"I could use a little cheering up," I said.

She pushed a bottle of wine and a glass across the counter. She already had a glass working.

"So, what's the trouble, Sherlock?" she said.

I told her about my ride with Rawlins, the visit to Bo's Berries, and the talk with Detective Jansson.

"I got a nice travelogue, a beginning helicopter lesson, and assurance that the cops are on the case," I said. "Not much new, though."

"How about those Phoenix murders?" Gabi asked.

"Big coincidence to swallow," I said. "Carla's playing coy about clients in Arizona at just the moment some illegal immigrants there get murdered."

"Have you asked her about it?"

"I want to learn more first," I said. "Otherwise, if there is a connection, she could just string me along."

"What are you going to do?"

"Tomorrow I'll go out to Riverside and see José Liebowitz's sister. Tomorrow night I'll fly home."

"What if I chain you to the bed?" Gabi said.

"Okay by me, but David Katz will get an injunction against you."

"An anti-restraining order," she said. "How come?"

"He needs me for an insurance deposition on Thursday afternoon. Friday I'll try to get with that Phoenix reporter who's covering the murders. Jenkins. You know him?"

"Tom Jenkins, sure. We met on lots of border stories when I worked in Tucson. I'll call to tell him you're coming, if you want."

"That would help," I said.

"You know," Gabi said, "he'll wonder what you're up to. Who hired you? What's the connection with the murders? Am I doing something on the murders? He's a nice guy, but this must be a huge story over there. He won't want to help someone who's going to beat him."

"I'll tell him I'm just an unimportant private eye without a clue," I said. "God knows that's true. You're not doing the story, are you?"

"There was talk today of sending someone, but you know the budget problems," she said. "I think they'll take the AP stuff unless a Southern California angle pops up."

"Those victims were probably coming here," I said. "If they were going to San Diego, they would have stopped in Tucson or Casa Grande. But a Phoenix layover usually means L.A."

"You know that and I know that," Gabi said. "But try telling it to some bean counter from Chicago."

She put the sliced tomatoes on two small plates. She cut canned hearts of palm into little sections and put them atop the tomatoes.

"Just like The Palm, but cheaper," she said. "And you get to sleep with the chef."

"Worth a special journey," I said.

"Check out those papers on the table," she said. "I ran a search on Carla and Rawlins before I came home."

I poured a glass of wine and sat at the small kitchen table. The Rawlins material was on top of the stacked printouts. A profile written several years earlier showed Rawlins standing by a helicopter. He had just won his first mediathon criminal trial, defending a Los Angeles police officer charged with unlawful use of force and involuntary manslaughter. Rawlins took the case for free. When he won, after a month of face time on television, his business boomed.

"Always try to defend a police officer," he told the reporter, "because then the cops will love you even when you defend pond scum later. I've had cops give my name to people they arrested. Sometimes I let firefighters borrow my helicopter if they need an extra one. They appreciate that and they show it. Arson investigators have recommended me to their suspects."

His time in the limelight must have been lucrative, but it was short. He apparently handed off most cases to young associates. His name faded from the papers a couple of years ago.

"Odd," Gabi said. "Big shot lawyers try to stay in the limelight."

"Some ego there," I said.

"That's what I thought," she said. "But he just sort of dropped out and let the kids do the work."

Gabi had included older clips from his divorce lawyer days. She even had a Westlaw search on his law review articles. His first was "All My Exes Live in Texas: A Comparison of Marital and Non-Marital Enforcement Actions Under the Interstate Child Support Compact."

"He likes country music, Gabi," I said. "He plays it in the helicopter. Even his legal writing uses song titles."

"You know why he does that?" Gabi said. "A law professor friend told me once. It's because the law review editors are students, and they love the pop culture references. It's an easy way to get published."

"Here's a good one," I said. "It's 'I Must Have Been Crazy, Boy, for Ever Loving You: Examining Mental Commitment Standards in California Domestic Units with Multiple Restraining Orders.' Is that a song?"

"Just the first part. Matraca Berg." She pronounced the middle syllable of Matraca like *trace*. "Huge talent. Writes for other stars and sings some herself."

"You like country now? Deserting our rock oldies?"

"Never," she said. "But it sounds like real music and the women are gutsy. Anyway, move along to the Carla stuff. Much more interesting than Rawlins."

The Times had interviewed Carla for a Sunday magazine story. She told the writer, "The beauty of immigration law is helping people who come here with nothing. They can become full partners in the American dream." That quote provided the article title, with a Karsh-quality portrait of Carla on the cover: "The Beauty of Immigration Law." Slick. I wondered how much a story like that was worth to a lawyer.

Gabi said, "It's a pretty standard puff piece. Mostly about Carla's being Latina herself, going to Harvard and Berkeley, wanting to open all that up to immigrants. It says she's very personal about her personal life. Not a word about Rawlins."

"Anything about her Tucson days?"

"Just that she was an honor student in high school after moving there from Albuquerque. You know how many hits you get when you Google Baca and Albuquerque? Three-hundred-forty-nine thousand. It's a big family name in New Mexico, apparently."

"Anything good?"

"One," she said. "It's right after the profile."

It was an Albuquerque newspaper story. I noticed the date: just a few months before Carla showed up at Tucson High.

CITY MAN CLAIMS BORDER PATROL BRUTALITY
by Lydia Dawes, Staff Writer

An Albuquerque man alleges in a federal court lawsuit that he was detained and beaten by Border Patrol agents during an immigration checkpoint stop near Hatch last month.

Carlos Baca, 38, was returning from an insurance sales call when he was stopped at the checkpoint on I-25, just north of Hatch, according to his lawsuit.

Baca said he showed the agents a New Mexico driver license, auto registration, and his business card, but the agents demanded a passport, birth certificate, or other proof of citizenship before they would allow him to proceed.

When Baca objected to the agents' action, his court papers claim, he was ordered out of his car, then taken to a spot behind the checkpoint trailer and beaten.

The lawsuit alleges that the agents called him a "dirty Mexican" and a "wetback" as they beat him. Baca says he suffered multiple cuts and bruises and a dislocated shoulder.

Baca's attorney, W. Elston Smythe of Albuquerque, showed a reporter Baca's United States passport, which listed his birthplace as Albuquerque.

"He didn't think he needed a passport to go to Hatch," Smythe said. "The Border Patrol apparently doesn't realize that New Mexico is not part of old Mexico."

Richard Jones, a spokesman for the Border Patrol's El Paso sector, said he was not able to comment on pending litigation.

Gabi said, "Did guys on the Patrol really do stuff like that?"

"We had a few bad agents," I said. "Pretty rare, though."

"I know," she said. "I never saw anything like that." Gabi had been on the border beat at the Tucson paper for a couple of years.

I held up the clipping and said, "That's Carla's father?"

"Got to be," Gabi said. "The profile said her late father Carlos was an insurance agent in Albuquerque. But the profile didn't mention the Border Patrol problem."

"I never heard this," I said. "I'll ask Al, but I don't think anyone at school knew about it."

"There were no other stories on the lawsuit," she said.

"That means they settled," I said. "Otherwise the Albuquerque papers would have stayed with it."

Carla put the steaks in the broiler and set a timer. She came to the table and sat across from me.

"That's what I figured. An incident like that might explain Carla's career choice, don't you think?"

"Getting even?"

"Maybe," Gabi said. "I know it sounds like amateur analysis again, but it's just what a smart, determined kid with a chip on her shoulder might do. Daddy gets beaten up by *la migra*, so daughter becomes Our Lady of the North and beats them up in court."

"Not that there's anything wrong with that," I said.

"No," she said, "but how driven is she? We know she wins by following the rules, using her legal skills and wily charms. What else would she do to beat the government?"

"Let's not get carried away," I said.

"Brinker," she said, "you're the one who's been wondering if there's something fishy about Carla and some connection to the Phoenix murders. I'm just following that thought."

"You're right," I said. "I'll follow it, too, when I get home."

"*Querida,*" she said, "you're home now. You just don't know it yet."

12

Gabi gave me her Thomas Guide maps, open to the section for San Bernardino, Riverside, and Redlands. I didn't know much about the place. Tucson runaways seldom ran to Riverside.

I did know that it's sixty miles east of Los Angeles and a world away from Hollywood. My auto club book said Riverside began life in the late 1800's as an agriculture town, famous for its orange groves. It has a state university campus and a famous old inn where Richard and Pat Nixon began their honeymoon. I forced from my mind the image of a honeymooning Nixon and hit the freeway.

Traffic was typical Southern California motor mania, bumper-to-bumper going seventy, then miles of stops and crawls. Lookie Lou's slowed near Hacienda Boulevard, watching the smoke that rose from the heights south of the freeway. I wished for Rawlins and his helicopter.

It took me two hours to reach Riverside. I got gasoline at a mini-mart and asked for directions to Sandra Liebowitz Brown's address. The bored young clerk had no clue. He offered to sell me a map for five dollars. I found the place myself in Gabi's big Thomas Guide. It was a couple of miles southeast of downtown.

The Browns' house sat on a small lot in a subdivision with well-watered lawns and tall palm trees lining the streets. If the sun ever broke through the smog, it would be a pretty place. The ranch style house was like most others on the block, one story of weathered wood and brick, with a big attached garage on the side. A blue Toyota Corolla was parked on the driveway. José Liebowitz's sister opened the front door before I could ring the bell.

"Mr. Brinker," she said, extending her hand. She looked more Mexican than her brother had, with thick hair, black going gray, cut to shoulder length, and a complexion of light golden brown. "Thank you for coming out. It's a long drive."

"I appreciate your talking to me," I said.

"I need to talk," she said. "I'm not exactly thrilled with the investigation so far."

She led me through the entry hall to the living room. Nothing fancy. There was a green fabric-covered sofa with a low coffee table in front of it. A matching fabric chair faced the sofa. Two recliners in brown Naugahyde were set for watching television.

"Would you like some coffee?" she asked. "Iced tea?"

"Iced tea would be perfect," I said. It was hot in Riverside, much hotter than Marina del Rey, and the air conditioning was off. She went to the kitchen and came back with a pitcher and two tall glasses filled with ice cubes. She put them on the coffee table and motioned me to the sofa. She took the chair and poured the iced tea.

"I'm glad you could come today," she said. "I teach third grade, just a few minutes from here. We're on summer vacation now, so I usually volunteer with local aid groups. But today I'm just taking some meals around to families at dinnertime. So this works out well for me."

"Why are you disappointed with the investigation?" I asked.

"Because there isn't one," she said. "Not really. A sheriff's detective called here to ask a few questions about Joseph. You know what they say about putting the victim on trial? That's exactly what it was like. Was he into drugs? Did he keep bad company? Deal with mobsters? Did he pick up prostitutes? I couldn't believe it."

"Well," I said, but she started in again.

"And that was it," she said. "One round of bullshit questions. Pardon me, Mr. Brinker. I'm mad. And on the phone he did this.

Just the phone. He didn't even come out here to talk to me. And nothing since. Not a follow up, not a report, nothing."

"Well," I said, "I didn't come to defend him, but those questions he asked are pretty standard in a murder case. You'd be surprised how often the answers help turn up a suspect."

"Fine," she said. "Start with that. But nothing else?"

"You're right," I said. "What do you think? Any ideas what happened?"

"Finally, somebody asks," she said. "Look, I'm just speculating, but when you don't have any real evidence, maybe speculation is okay?"

"Yes," I said.

She took a sip of iced tea and said, "Joseph kept lots of cash. He had it in the house and his car. He did that because he was suspicious of credit cards. You know, I.D. theft is such a problem now. And he liked to have money to show his clients. He paid their bar bills and overtipped their porters, that kind of thing. He used to say showbiz people had to do that to keep up appearances."

"The detectives have his bank accounts. I don't think they've actually done any digging on that yet."

"Of course they haven't," she said.

"Did you tell them about his keeping cash on hand?"

"I tried. But by the time it occurred to me, they weren't returning my calls. I guess they figured I was just a pest."

"Did he have an attorney, besides Carla?" I asked. "Who's handling the estate?"

"I'm the personal administrator, of course," she said. "I'm Joseph's only surviving relative. The attorney handling probate was Joseph's personal attorney and accountant. His name is Norton Silber. He has an office in West L.A. I can give you one of his business cards."

"Have you gone through his personal things? I'm wondering about address books or date books that might provide some new lead."

"The police took a while to release the apartment and its contents," she said. "I'm still looking through things. He had one of those weekly calendar books with a place at the end for addresses and phone numbers. He had a laptop computer with a calendar and address book, too. I've looked at them, but they didn't tell me anything. I can give you those, if you like."

"I'd appreciate that," I said. "The attorney, Mr. Silber. Has he mentioned any unusual cash movements before your brother died? Large withdrawals or unexplained checks?"

She shook her head. "It's a small estate. Joseph didn't have a huge business, you know. He lived comfortably, and had savings. He gave me a little money for charity work when I asked. But basically he was going from month to month, like the rest of us. Mr. Silber has told me about the general estate. I've signed some checks when he asked me to. Court fees, Joseph's last bills, that kind of thing. But I haven't talked with him much about the particulars of Joseph's money."

"I'd like to," I said.

"I'll call him today," she said. "If you have my permission, there should be no problem."

"Thank you," I said. "You know, Mrs. Brown, some of those cop questions can be helpful. Did your brother have any romantic problems? Anybody mad at him?"

"He dated a couple of women," she said. "Joseph said neither one expected anything serious. I didn't get the sense that those relationships were ever intense. And he never mentioned trouble with anyone."

"Any drug issues?" I asked, remembering Jansson's hints.

"Nothing big, as far as I know. He must have done some marijuana, like everyone else," she said. She gave me a sly smile.

"You call him Joseph," I said.

"He was always Joseph since he was a baby," she said. "The José thing, that was Hollywood stuff. Kind of a stage name."

I stood to leave. "I'll call you as soon as I learn anything," I said.

"Wait just a moment," she said. She left the room and returned quickly with and black soft-cover appointment book, a white laptop computer, and a handful of white cords. I thanked her.

"By the way," I said, "have you been asked about your brother's death by anyone else? Someone besides the cops and me?"

"No," she said.

"I was wondering if some people who work for Carla were working on this. O'Laughlin Security Services."

"If they are," she said, "they haven't spoken to me."

I opened the front door. "Thank you again," I said. "I'm very sorry about your brother."

"He changed his name legally, you know," she said. "There's nothing wrong with it. I changed my last name when I married. That was what people did then. I wouldn't do it now. Don't you think it's strange that we can change actual facts about ourselves?

"I see it all the time," I said. "Changing a name is harmless compared to what some people do to themselves."

"What a terrible job you must have," she said, extending her hand, looking genuinely sorry for me.

13

It was after one o'clock when I reached downtown L.A. Two hours out to Riverside, one hour there, ninety minutes back. No wonder that Detective Jansson had called Sandra Brown instead of driving out. How did anybody get any work done in the clogged arteries of this town?

I left the freeway at Alameda and followed the signs to Union Station. What I really wanted was a French dip sandwich at Phillipe the Original, up the street. Phillipe is one of several joints that claim to have invented the French dip. I can't confirm the history but I like the food and the unpretentious old-timeyness.

The place was surrounded by cop cars. I lucked into a space in the parking lot and entered through the side door on Ord. The restaurant wasn't a crime scene. The cops were there for lunch. About twenty uniformed officers sat at the long wooden tables, shuffling the sawdust on the floor with their spit-shined shoes, eating sandwiches and cole slaw and drinking coffee or soda. I felt safe.

The restaurant looked exactly as I remembered it from coming here with my dad years ago. We sometimes drove over from Tucson for a weekend at Dodger Stadium or an Arizona football game against USC at the Coliseum. Ladies in tan dresses with green collar trim still worked behind the big glass cases, making sandwiches and serving up sides and pie and drinks. Same ladies, maybe. Nothing changed much here. I got a beef dip and a lemonade and took a seat next to a couple of cops who looked about fifteen years old.

Phillipe is the non-showbiz part of Los Angeles in microcosm. Cops of all races, but mostly Hispanic. Young managers from the downtown office towers, cell phones in hand, mingled with teenage Mexican girls and their grandmothers. Construction guys, maybe from projects at Union Station or the post office. Old people, poor, probably, but with a few bucks for a sandwich and plenty of time to eat it. At least a dozen men and women, mostly Anglo, wore Dodger shirts and caps. The Cubs were visiting this afternoon at Chavez Ravine, just a mile or so away. Tempting. José Liebowitz probably liked ball games and funky L.A. hangouts, too, I thought. That snapped my mind back to Carla's case.

Norton Silber answered his own phone and told me to come on over. Yes, Sandra Brown had called him and he would be happy to talk to me about the José Liebowitz estate. He said to take the 101 to the 405, because Wilshire was impossible at midday. I finished my sandwich and reluctantly crept back into the unrelenting traffic.

Silber's office was on the ground floor of a small professional building on Westwood Avenue, too far south of Wilshire to be a sterling Westside address. Silber himself met me in the reception room. He was not quite six feet tall. His body and his hair were painfully thin. He was the last guy west of downtown L.A. still wearing a starched white shirt and a necktie. It was black knit, skinny, like lawyers sported on fifties television shows, or Edward James Olmos's character wore on Miami Vice.

"My secretary called in sick," he said, leading me back to his office. "I wish I could. Have a seat, Mr. Brinker." He looked strictly business. There would be no Colombian coffee or high school banter here.

"I wonder if you know of anything in José Liebowitz's affairs that might have figured in his death," I said.

"No," Silber said. "José's financial affairs and business affairs were quite regular. A bit more cash dealing than many people, but all in order and nothing extraordinary about them."

"His sister told me that he kept a lot of cash around," I said.

"That's true," Silber said. "But again, there's nothing unusual about that, especially for people in his line of work. Even in this age of credit cards, people often use cash for entertaining. José said it was also helpful for arrangements in theaters and clubs where his clients worked."

"Arrangements. What did that mean, do you suppose?"

"I supposed that a little cash bonus payment helped with the occasional labor issue, or emergency repairs of musical equipment. Other things that might come up in the world of performance."

"Like?"

"Well," Silber said, "I'm naïve about these things. But José gave me to believe that performers sometimes need, um, supplies that are not available at conventional retail sources."

"Uh-oh," I said.

Silber just nodded.

I said, "Was he shopping for drugs around the time he died?"

"I wasn't his chaperone," the attorney said. "I'm just relaying what he told me, in pretty much his exact words."

"Did he use?" I asked.

"Never in my presence, obviously," Silber said. "Furthermore, I never observed any signs of abuse by José."

"Tell me about the cash," I said. "Could you track it on his bank records?"

"Sandra asked me to do just that and to tell you what I found. This is more information than I would ever give out without permission, but I'm acting at the request of the personal administrator."

"And?"

"And," Silber said, "he withdrew one-thousand dollars a week for the last six weeks of his life."

"This is over and above regular expenses like rent and car payments and such?"

"Exactly. José usually picked up a hundred dollars at the ATM every week or so. Maybe more if he was hosting a client for a few days, but seldom a thousand dollars until that last period of time."

"Any clients around for those last six weeks?"

Silber consulted a folder that lay open on his desk.

"One, during the third week," he said. "It was a one-night appearance by a Mexican guitarist at a small venue on the UCLA campus. Quite distinguished, apparently. A Segovia type of guitarist. I remember that José mentioned the gentleman had family in Sherman Oaks and planned to spend most of his time with them. Not the sort of client with high overhead or a cocaine habit, I imagine."

He closed the folder and pushed it across the desk to me.

"Copies of bank statements, last two income tax returns, personal and business, the will," he said. "I hope this is helpful somehow. I want to remind you that I'm providing this in confidence at Sandra's request."

"Thank you," I said. "I was wondering, did you ever do any work with Carla Baca?"

"Never had the pleasure," he said. "Her practice is limited to immigration, I understand. Why is her own investigator asking me that?"

"Insatiable curiosity," I said.

"Well, I've seen Ms. Baca on television," he said. "I can understand the insatiable part." I swear that he almost smiled a thin little smile. I semi-smiled back.

"Where are you headed now?" he asked.

"LAX," I said. Gabi had gone to Anaheim for a story and wouldn't be home until late, so I planned to head straight to the airport.

"I'd go down Sepulveda and take Century or Imperial west," he said. "The 405 and the Santa Monica will be impossible by now."

14

David Katz gives me office space at his law firm. It's a respectable place to meet clients. Even better, David carries me on the Alejandro & Katz books as a regular employee with group medical. Guys who might occasionally get shot have trouble finding private health insurance, so I'm grateful. If David wants me in town on Thursday afternoon, I'll be there on Wednesday night to keep him happy and reassured.

"We're on at 1:30 tomorrow," David said when I called him from baggage claim at Tucson airport. "I still hope this will settle, so keep your phone on tomorrow morning. If we scrap the deposition, I'll let you know before your whole day is wasted."

My part of the office deal is handling a few insurance investigations. David represents insurance companies. They're dislikable villains, but someone is always trying to scam them. My deposition was needed in the case of one Matilda Griswold of Tucson, who claimed to have suffered painful injuries when the SunTran bus in which she was riding hit another bus at the Tohono Transit Center.

David set up my deposition so that Ms. Griswold would already have been deposed under oath, complaining of reckless bus drivers speeding through the station, putting her life and limb at risk. Then I would come in, bearing the SunTran videotape that runs 24/7 at all stations. A friend of mine from Tucson High set up the security system. I called him when David told me about the lawsuit. My friend said he would dig up the tape from the time of the accident. Meanwhile, he asked me to get a subpoena as a CYA measure. David got it, and the tape was waiting when I went to pick it up.

The tape showed one slow-moving bus nudging another, causing a dent and some scraped paint, but prompting no other claim of debilitating injuries. It also showed Ms. Griswold standing in line for another bus at the time of the low-speed collision. Ms. Griswold, evidently a first-time grifter, obviously didn't know about the cameras.

"Thanks to such silly souls, we earn our daily bread," David said. And at 7:30 the next morning, he called to say that he and Ms. Griswold's attorney, given a clue about my pending deposition, had agreed that she would drop her claim.

"You're letting her walk?" I asked.

"No charges need be filed or jail time sought, I think," David said. "Her name will be entered in the eternally damning database of all leading insurers. If she's that foolish again, she'll set off alarm bells from here to Hartford. I hope you have something better to do with your day."

"Oh, yeah," I said.

I called Thomas Jenkins at the Phoenix AP. He was already at work. When I dropped Gabi's name, he agreed to meet me at the bureau in the Viad Tower on North Central Avenue.

The interstate was clear and I made good time until I hit the southern suburb of Chandler. From that point, Phoenix seemed to be emulating L.A. The traffic lurched from crazy fast to stop-and-go.

The Viad Tower stood twenty-four stories tall. A soap company built it. Legend has it that the top floor was designed to look like a bar of soap. Where was Howard Roark when they really needed him? Its exterior reflects the natural light, giving it a spectacular red glow at sunset. On this gray summer morning, it looked like just another office building packed with tycoons and drones. I found the AP offices on the sixth floor.

Thomas Jenkins was a slight, thirty-something guy in a white wash-and-wear shirt, seldom washed and often worn. He completed the ensemble with rumpled chinos and house brand hiking shoes from Wal-Mart. I'll bet Phoenix newsmakers underestimate him until his stories come out.

When I found his cubicle, he was talking on the phone, using a hands-free headset while he typed on a computer keyboard.

"Okay, thanks, Lieutenant," he said. He pulled off the headset and saw me. "You Gabi's friend?"

"My only claim to fame," I said. We shook hands.

"Not exactly," he said. "You were there when Nogales caught fire a few years ago."

"No fair checking your files," I said.

He laughed. "Call a reporter, take your chances," he said. "So, what's your interest in the shootings?"

"I have a client who works in immigration," I said. "Naturally, something like this caught her attention."

"Naturally," Jenkins said. "Who's your client?"

"Now, now," I said.

"Oh, yeah, the old 'protecting your source' trick," he said. "Gabi's not going to parachute in here and use the stuff I tell you?"

"No," I said. "Her paper sent her to Anaheim yesterday, so the travel budget is shot for this month."

"Jeez, isn't that the truth," he said. "Cutbacks are killing this business. Well, I was just talking to a source of mine at the cop shop. The theory of the case seems to change every fifteen minutes or so."

"What's the current consensus?" I said.

"Gangland clash," Jenkins said. "We know that all kinds of smuggler rings operate out of the Mexican border towns. That includes people smuggling. The folks who want to go north pay in advance. The *coyotes* pile everyone in a van or a cargo crate or whatever and take them. Sometimes it's just over the border, but usually it's to a destination city like Phoenix or L.A. where jobs are available."

"Tougher now, with the workplace crackdowns," I said.

He shrugged. "Yeah, but lots of these illegals have friends or relatives here who can steer them to employers that look the other way. In Arizona and California, there's lots of construction and landscaping work. No way the G can keep track of it all."

"Okay," I said. "What about the clash?"

"Smuggling people into the states is big business now," he said.

"The fees can be thousands of dollars. There's tens of thousands of customers. So it's getting to be like drugs. The bad guys are fighting for turf."

"They kill the customers of rival gangs?"

"That's the theory." Jenkins leaned back and laced his fingers behind his head and tugged, stretching his neck muscles.

"Doesn't make sense," I said. "Why kill the customers? Why not just kill the other gang members, then tell the customers, We'll get you to L.A. or wherever for another thousand dollars."

"I'm just a humble reporter, relaying what the people in power tell me," he said. "The cops think maybe it's to put fear on the streets in Mexico. Make new customers scared to choose Gang A instead of Gang B."

That gave me an idea, but I kept it to myself.

"Have they made all the ID's yet?" I asked.

"Most of them," he said.

"Any surprises?"

"No. There is one weird thing, though. The cops found old fast food trash in the house. Lots of coffee cups, but one little half pint milk carton."

"I didn't read anything about a kid."

"There wasn't anything," he said. "All the victims there were adults. It's not like an adult was drinking milk, because the *coyotes* don't take food orders. They just bring in some food and say, 'eat this.' There were more coffee cups in the room than there were bodies."

"That's why the cops think other people were in that room," I said.

"Exactly," Jenkins said. "And they're thinking, maybe one of the adults had a little kid. That kid is either dead somewhere else, or somebody out there has got it."

"You can't sell an adult, but you could sell a child," I said.

"Some business plan, huh?" he said. "Make the people pay in advance, get them here, kill them, steal their kid."

"That can't be the plan," I said. "Most people don't bring children when they sneak in. Something went wrong. Maybe an unexpected scrap of decency kept them from killing a child. Or they saw an opportunity to sell this one."

We were silent for a while. Jenkins took a business card from his shirt pocket and gave it to me.

"I don't know what you're doing, exactly," he said. "Out of respect for Gabi, I'm not going to worry about it. But if you come up with anything interesting, I'd appreciate a little reciprocity."

"You got it," I said.

I called Gabi's cell. When she answered, I said, "I miss you."

"Oh, boy," she said. "For a tough guy, you're getting awfully good with the sweet talk."

"Maybe we could split the difference on living together," I said. "You can live in L.A. and I can live in Tucson. We could meet halfway, like a motel in Blythe." It's a famously unglamorous town near the California-Arizona border.

"The worst of both worlds," she said.

"I'm going to Nogales tomorrow," I said. "If anybody knows something about the current state of people smuggling, it's Hector. Then I'll square off with Carla on Monday. See you Monday night?

"I'll iron the apron," Gabi said.

15

When I was on the Border Patrol, I rescued a Mexican kid in a dry wash near Rio Rico, about fifteen miles north of the border. Two thugs were beating him so viciously that I was sure they had murder in mind. After I chased off the attackers, I realized I knew their victim because I had seen him play baseball in Tucson. High schools there imported Mexican kids to strengthen their teams.

The young shortstop was Hector Ortiz. After high school, he got tryouts with the Dodgers and Padres, but couldn't make it. He went back to Mexico and became a drug dealer. Now he's a kingpin, as the newspapers say, in Nogales, Sonora. That makes him an influential citizen there.

He still thinks he owes me for driving away his attackers in that wash. I still use him.

I parked by the old Nogales train station on the Arizona side and walked to the border. You leave the United States through a narrow walled walk that ends at a one-way revolving gate. It's the flip side of Hotel California: you can check out but you can't check back in. For that, you must circle around to the U.S. immigration station. I took a deep breath and pushed through the gate.

Tourists and locals lined up at Hector's restaurant on the Avenida Obregón. The buffet lunch was a big draw. As I approached the line, Hector's man Vicente stepped out from a doorway and took my arm. Vicente is a big, solid guy, built like a wide receiver. When he takes your arm, you don't fight it.

"This way," he said. He led down an alley that took us to the rear of the restaurant. He pointed to the back door and said, "Into the kitchen, up the stairs on the right. I'll just stay here for a while, make sure nobody tagged along."

The aromas of *chilaquiles* and *mole* hit me as entered the kitchen. I wanted to stop and sample everything. A man at the foot of the stairs stood aside and said, "*Le espera.*" He's waiting.

I hadn't seen Hector for almost three years. He looked tired. His black Pancho Villa moustache had taken on specks of gray. It drooped to exaggerate the fatigue. Hector sat at a table against the far wall of the small office. He didn't get up. We didn't shake hands.

"Been a while," he said. "The charms of old Mexico don't lure you down here anymore?"

I took a chair across the table from him.

"How are Frida and María?" I said.

"Best I have," he said. Frida and María were former *maquiladora* employees who had helped me investigate the murders of several fellow workers. When the case ended and their factory burned down, Hector gave them jobs in the restaurant.

"They're still living with Vicente?" I asked.

Hector laughed. "Vicente. I don't know how he does it. I'd be in a coma."

"I've got a problem, Hector."

"Really?" he said. "When did you ever come down here without a problem?"

"You hear about the murders up in Phoenix?"

"The people in the house by the airport."

"Right."

"Sure," he said. "Nobody talked about anything else for a few days after that."

I waited for more, but it wasn't Hector's style to volunteer everything at once.

"The cops think it might have been a rival gang thing," I said. "One gang wants to scare potential customers away from doing business with the other gang."

He shook his head. "Who thought up that shit?" he said. "How are the customers going to find out? It's not like smugglers put up signs. 'Come with us and we won't kill you.' No, it's all sweet talk. 'You got the money? Hand it over and we'll get you where you want to go.' Besides, the customers come from all over Mexico, Guatemala, wherever. They don't know who's bad and who's good. They just know where to show up and ask for guides."

"Where's that, these days?"

"Sásabe was good, but *la migra* has that pretty choked up right now. San Luis, by Yuma, that's getting tougher every day. They have more lights there than Dodger Stadium. National Guardsmen from Tennessee patrolling all over the place, looking out for Mexicans. You guys aren't being very good neighbors."

"What about you, Hector?"

"You're not listening, my friend. I'm just a businessman, and that business isn't very good right now. Fewer people trying to cross because of the crackdowns. When you do get a customer, it's too much risk for too little return."

"What do you mean, fewer people?" I said. "Pima County had ninety bodies in the morgue last week."

"Last week is last week," Hector said. "Some of those bodies were out there for a long time. They don't tell us what's happening now, let alone tomorrow. I'm concerned about tomorrow."

"A reporter in Phoenix told me it's big business," I said.

Hector smiled. "If you rely on reporters for news about Mexico, you'll always be six months behind."

"So?"

"So, I'm telling you that things are changing. Tomorrow's business prospects in international relocation are not good."

Vicente had come in and closed the door behind him quietly. I didn't know he was there until he spoke. Vicente is like that.

"For one thing," he said, "the climate is changing. States are passing immigration laws. There's pressure on businesses. INS is raiding places they've known about for years, and now they get serious."

"Plus," Hector said, "all the sheriffs want to get TV time, so they have raids and drag out a few Mexicans."

I said, "People still want to go, though."

"Yeah, but then we have some practical problems, too," Vicente said. "Say a man weighs sixty kilos. He gives you three thousand dollars to take him from Sásabe to Los Angeles. You guide him across the border on foot, then you gotta have a van or something to take him and other customers the rest of the way. And if you do it right, you need somebody watching the Border Patrol so you know what roads to avoid. Maybe a U.S. citizen in a clean car driving ahead to be sure there's no roadblocks or cruising intercepts. So you're spending a lot to get your three thousand, even with a vanload of customers."

Hector said, "Wouldn't it make more sense, if we're going to risk it, to take sixty kilos of something else across the border?"

"Something else," I said.

"Yeah," Vicente said. "Think of anything?"

"One kilo, three-hundred grand," I said. "Sixty kilos, wow."

"Eighteen million bucks worth of wow," Vicente said.

"Vicente is very quick at math," Hector said. "One of his great values to me."

"So you're out of the people business," I said.

"I never said I was in it," Hector said. "If I was, though, I'd be mostly out now. If anybody still does that, it's a sideline." A little smile formed beneath the big moustache.

"Who's in?" I said.

Hector just stared at me. The smile got bigger.

"Who wants to know?" he said.

"My client works with immigrants," I said. "I'm wondering if he's involved somehow with the people who got killed in Phoenix." Saying "he" was a little lie, but Hector and I take small liberties with each other.

Hector thought about it for a moment. He kept looking hard into my eyes. That stare must have frightened a few men over the years.

"Vicente," he said, "bring a bottle over here and sit down. Let's all have a drink."

Vicente took the Cuervo Gold from a cupboard and brought it with three small glasses. None of the salt and lime hoo-hah like they served the restaurant customers. Vicente poured. We each drank the shot. Vicente poured again.

"So," Hector said. "Works with immigrants, huh?"

I nodded.

"That means," Hector said, "that your client is a do-gooder group that helps people get across or helps them when they arrive. Or maybe somebody who helps them work the legal system."

My turn to wait and say nothing.

Hector said, "Do-gooder groups don't hire private eyes. Lawyers do, though. And if the people are undocumented, as you say up there, and the lawyer is helping them sneak in, then that means your lawyer client is a crook, according to the highly-evolved legal and ethical standards of the United States."

I took another sip of tequila. Hector downed his glassful in one shot.

"You sure know how to pick 'em, *amigo*," he said.

Vicente said, "Think about this. You want to kill a bunch of people, why would you take them to Phoenix first? Wouldn't it make more sense, be more economical, to take them out in the desert? Someplace near the border, maybe on this side. No death penalty here, for starters."

"Killing people anywhere makes no sense to me," I said.

"Spare me," Vicente said. "You've put a few down."

"Arizona police and Border Patrol are a little more likely to be a pain in the ass than our guys here," Hector said. "Here, it's easier for arrangements to be made. And if those killings are tied to immigrant smuggling, you've got a federal offense. That means the FBI."

"Or some kind of Homeland Security blitz," Vicente said. "Either way, if you're in business, killing people in the states don't make sense. Even killing the competition's customers is stupid. People who want to go north, they say it was bad enough with the rattlesnakes and the sun. Now we've got drug warfare to survive, too. Let's just stay home until things cool down."

"What do you mean, drug war?" I said.

Hector said, "Let's say, just for example, that you're shipping some kind of product north. And let's say you don't want the Border Patrol and all the other U.S. agencies interfering with this shipment."

"They've got so many agents out there now," Vicente said. "The only way to keep them out of your business is to point them at something else."

I thought about it, but Hector stood up before I could speak.

"Like I say," he said, "the immigrant smuggling business by itself doesn't interest me at all. I think that's enough information for today."

"Keep your ears open," I said. I stood to leave. Vicente was already by the door, ready to take me downstairs.

Hector said, "You want, I could give Frida and María a couple of hours off. One at a time, though, 'cause we're busy on Sundays."

"No, thanks," I said. "Wouldn't they rather be with you, Hector?"

Hector laughed. "Not me, *hermano*. Vicente wouldn't let me."

I turned to Vicente and asked, "You're jealous?"

"No," he said. "It's my job to keep Hector alive."

The U.S. Customs agent at the pedestrian Port of Entry looked at my white face and blue passport. If my name was on a list somewhere, he didn't care. He asked me if I bought anything in Mexico. I said no and he waved me through. The Mexican family behind me got more questions, but in a minute I heard them laughing happily and talking about Big Macs and fries as they came out behind me on the American side.

My parking place near the train station had caught the summer sun for most of the early afternoon. The car would be an oven. I started the engine and turned on the air conditioner. I was about to get out and let the interior cool for a few minutes when I looked toward the motor vehicle Port of Entry.

A Lincoln Town Car with Arizona plates had just come through the security area. It stopped on Grand Avenue, waiting to turn left. The passenger, a woman, spoke with animation to her male driver. I could hear nothing, but she was gesturing and seemed to be shouting. The driver said nothing. Oblivious to me, they turned and headed for I-19. I eased into traffic and onto the freeway ramp. I hung back for almost sixty miles, letting them stay several vehicles ahead.

Just south of San Xavier Road, my cell phone rang. I usually ignore it when I'm driving, but the display showed Vicente's number.

"The boss wants you to think about our conversation," Vicente said. "He thinks maybe you missed the point."

"The only point I got was that you guys aren't in that business these days," I said. "It's people intensive and not worth the hassle."

"The boss was right," Vicente said. He hung up.

A couple of cars had moved into my lane. I pulled out to pass them and close the gap with the Town Car. As I expected, it turned off at Valencia, taking Carla Baca and Richard Rawlins toward the Tucson airport.

16

"You have a nice weekend?" I asked.

Carla and I sat in her office. Monday, just before noon. She was at her desk. I took the client chair. The view down Wilshire Boulevard spread out behind her. The sun was high but smog colored the sunlight in that bright gray unique to L.A. The radio announcers had warned of heavy air pollution because of a stationary front over the basin and the fires in La Habra Heights.

"Very nice, thanks," Carla said. Her smile was easy and her eyes twinkled with no apparent guile.

"Gabi says there's lots to do every weekend here," I said. "Not like our sleepy old Tucson."

"You should move here," she said. "You'd have a pretty girl friend and beach apartment already. Licensing would be no problem, given your experience. You'd get good work in a hurry. What more could you want?"

"Hard to leave my hometown after all these years," I said. "It's a good place, and Mexico's so close."

Nothing.

"Well," Carla said after a moment, "how are you doing on the cases?"

"There's no connection I can find between José Liebowitz and Bo Bergstrom, except that you represented them on immigration issues," I said.

"That worries me," she said. "That I'm the connection, I mean."

"I think the L.A. sheriff's homicide people are doing what they can. That detective, Jansson, he seems sharp."

"He hates me," Carla said. "He thinks I'm just a little affirmative action confection. An agitator."

"I wouldn't say he hates you," I said.

"He likes my butt," she said. "Every time I see him, I catch him staring. Can you believe that? It's the twenty-first century and professional women still have to put up with that crap."

"Well, you're a twenty-first century fox," I said.

"Oh, please, not you, too," she said, but she laughed anyway.

"Carla," I said, "the Arizona case is about the people murdered in Phoenix, right?"

She had a good lawyer poker face. She held my stare and kept her small smile.

"All right," she said.

"You told me that somebody is killing your clients. You said three cases. Two here in California, one in Arizona. That means Liebowitz, Bergstrom, and those people in Phoenix."

"Which means what?" she said.

"You're agreeing in advance to represent people that you know are breaking the law," I said. "If they were your clients, it had to be arranged before they got here."

"That's ridiculous," she said. "Do you think I'm a complete idiot?"

"Right now," I said, "I don't know what to think."

Her face colored. She could take public criticism in the newspapers and conflict in court, but Carla was not accustomed to being challenged in person. I thought of Richard Rawlins saying, "She's a little turbulent."

"Look," she said. "If I'm facilitating illegal entrances, that's a federal offense. Even if I beat that, I'd still be jammed up with the bar association if I were doing it to get clients. There would be no way to keep that secret. Look at me. Look at this practice. You think some jealous or malicious jerk wouldn't rat me out in a heartbeat?"

"So what's the deal, Carla?" I said. "What's your connection with that horror show in Phoenix?"

"Okay," she said. She pushed some papers around her desk and dug through a stack. She pulled out a sheet of lined paper and passed it across the desk to me. It was a letter, written in pencil, in Spanish.

"Dear Miss Baca," it said, "my name is Enrique Martinez. I live in Ensenada, Baja California, Mexico. I want to come to the United States to work and earn money for my family. I am a good worker and very honest. My friends in Los Angeles say you are a lawyer who helps many people. Please write to tell me how I can come to your country." The letter had a return address and a number for a friend in Ensenada who had a telephone.

Carla said, "I get five to ten of those every week. I have a form letter that I send back with contact information for my associated firm in Tijuana. I tell the people to contact that firm for immigration information and for starting the visa process, if they want to do that. Once they're here, if they have problems, I can help at this end."

"Okay," I said.

"One-hundred percent totally okay," Carla said. "I'm not practicing law in Mexico, where I have no license. I'm not soliciting in California because they contacted me, not the other way around. I'm not counseling anyone to violate federal law. I refer them to a bona fide firm in Mexico to arrange legal entry."

"What about Phoenix?" I said.

She looked exasperated. "That's what I'm telling you, Brinker. Two weeks ago, I got a letter like that from a woman in Guaymas, Sonora. The same thing about her friends saying I can help. But this one didn't ask for information. It just said, 'My husband and my baby and I are traveling through Nogales, and then to Los Angeles. When I arrive, I'll call you for help with getting papers.' She just signed her name. No address or phone. I couldn't get back to her."

"What would you have said?"

"I'd have said forget it," Carla said. "If I offered help, that would have been proof that I'm telling Mexicans to break United States law now and we'll fix it later. Totally unacceptable. I've got a form letter for that, too, but I couldn't reply to this woman."

She seemed to be wiggling around behind her desk. I figured that she was working in stocking feet and trying to slip into her heels.

"So," I said, "when you heard about the Phoenix mess, you figured she might have been one of the victims."

"Exactly," Carla said. "Everybody knows that Phoenix is a stopping point for undocumented immigrants coming from Sonora to L.A."

"But you told me, 'Someone is killing my clients.' Why did you say that if this woman wasn't even a client?"

Carla stood and put her hands up to her face, as if to say, someone please save me from this moron. She had the heels on, for sure.

"Brinker, do I have to draw a diagram for you? I had two murdered clients who were connected by nothing except my being their lawyer. Now a houseful of people gets slaughtered, and maybe one of them had been in contact with me. Wouldn't you want to know if that woman was in that house? And if so, was her death somehow connected to José and Bo?"

"Did you find out?"

She sighed and sank back into her chair.

"No," she said. "I tried. The Phoenix cops won't talk to me. Amric worked the phone for two days. He talked to INS and some friendly reporters. I called a man I knew in Albuquerque who's an FBI agent in Phoenix now. Nobody knows anything."

I thought of Terry O'Laughlin and his disdainful smirk.

"You want me on it?" I said.

"Of course. Don't ignore the two murders here, but certainly find out what you can about Phoenix."

"What was the woman's name?" I said.

Carla fumbled around in the papers and came up with a notepad. She wrote a name on the top sheet, tore it off, and pushed it across the desk.

"Lourdes Ortega," I said. "Nobody in that house has been identified yet. I don't even know if any women were killed. But the cops will have to release some names soon."

Carla nodded. She turned away and looked out the big window. She seemed deflated, far from the self-confident world beater I had met here a week ago.

"You sure you still want me on this, Carla?" I said. "If you're been playing loose with the law, it'll come back to bite you."

"Do your damn job," she said, surveying the city beneath her.

17

A small coffee shop occupied about half of the ground floor lobby of Carla's office building. When I arrived an hour earlier, a man had been sitting at a tiny square table reading the Times sports page. I noticed because it featured an article about a University of Arizona basketball player who was expected to be next year's number one NBA draft choice. When I came downstairs, the sports fan was still there, still on the same page.

I walked around the corner to a Starbucks on Sixth. I needed a caffeine hit, anyway. Carla hadn't offered Colombian coffee this morning. I ordered, chatted with the cheerful black barista while she made my coffee, and took a seat by the window.

The guy from Carla's building wandered in. What a surprise. He asked the barista for a small latte. She gave him a sunny lecture about how "tall" is the new small. The guy took his coffee to a table across the room from me. He sat down and opened the sports section to the NBA draft story. Not a speed-reader.

Someone had left a copy of the Times on the table next to mine. I grabbed it and spent a few minutes learning about high parking rates in the central business district, a Guatemalan-American running for state assembly, and a pop music star who spent very little money on underwear.

Occasionally I glanced over at my shadow and fixed his face in my memory. Hispanic, mid-twenties, hair cut very short all around. Nice looking guy, the kind that every *abuela* hopes her granddaughter will marry. He was tailing me, so I figured him for a crook, but he didn't look the part. No barrio gangster bullshit, no bling, no visible tattoos. He wore business casual black slacks, a long-sleeved black silk shirt, and nicely shined black loafers. He had a tiny cell phone holstered on his belt. He looked like a thousand other young up-and-comers on the streets of downtown L.A. No place that I could see to conceal a gun.

I put aside the paper, picked up my cup, and headed for the door. The barista said, "Have a great day, honey." I waved and stepped outside. I walked back along Sixth, no hurry, sipping my coffee.

When I turned the corner at Hope, the guy was at the edge of my vision, strolling along behind. I entered the lobby of Carla's building and made for the elevators. I pressed the Parking Level 2 button and stepped back, facing outside. I spotted the guy standing at the curb, watching the street.

The Times story was right about high parking rates. I gave the attendant a twenty and got coins back. When I drove up the ramp onto Hope, my new friend was slipping into the passenger seat of a Ford sedan that stopped in the curb lane. A cell phone call to a driver circling the block, I figured. My shadow was pretty obvious but he played for a team. Somebody was serious about following me.

Okay, I thought. Let's see how far they push it.

I twisted around a couple of blocks to Eighth and got on the 110 Freeway toward Pasadena. The tails lagged two cars behind. North of the massive interchange, traffic lightened. I floored it and did seventy-five for a mile.

At the Dodger Stadium exit, I swung off and headed for the ticket office. My followers must be baseball fans, too. They were still with me, hanging back nicely. No game today, so they couldn't lose themselves in a mob of fans' cars.

This should be the safest place in L.A. to get out of my car. Dodger Stadium is next door to the Los Angeles Police Academy. LAPD was supposed to be moving its training operations to the west side, but squad cars and unmarkeds still came and went from the Academy constantly. I wondered if my tails knew that. Their Ford sedan was just like mine, brand new, clean, tan. It could be a rental like mine. These guys could be out-of-towners.

When I pulled into Lot P, the tails kept going. I walked to the ticket office and studied the schedule. Giants in town next week. Maybe Gabi and I could catch a game. I took a ticket information packet and headed back to my car. Only a few stadium vehicles were in sight. An SUV had pulled in and parked in the shade of a California pepper tree at the edge of the lot.

I drove around the parking lot loop. I got lucky. The Dodgers had left the gates open, so it was easy to pick up Academy Drive. The street goes north for a quarter-mile or so, then bends east. A nice cover of shrubs and trees stood between me and the stadium parking lot. I ducked into the Academy entrance road and drove up the palm-lined street. I slipped into the parking lot next to an RV. The spot gave me cover and a perfect view of Academy Drive. I waited.

It took only fifteen seconds for the SUV to swing east on Academy Drive. Only the driver inside, a man I hadn't spotted before. He couldn't see my car on the long straightway. He must have assumed that I sped up to lose him, so he took it up to seventy and roared past. I got the plate.

Sometimes, life is perfect.

A squad car came around the Academy Drive curve just as the SUV driver punched it. I started to laugh even before the cops hit the flashers and siren. The black-and-white barreled after the SUV and turned out of sight on Solano Avenue. A moment later, the siren wound down. I pulled out and headed for the freeway. The cops were approaching the SUV, one walking on each side in classic traffic stop position.

I wanted to wave as I drove by, but it would be better if he didn't know I had made him. When I looked in my rear view mirror, the driver was handing over his license.

18

Gabi said, "Three guys?"

"Three that I know about," I said.

We were at her apartment. I sat close to the balcony, keeping an eye on the sidewalks and a sliver of visible parking area. I felt confident that nobody had followed me here, but if they were good, I wouldn't know.

"Why don't we go to Hawaii?" she said. "Hide out in some nice hotel. Spend a couple of hours on the beach, then go undercover, so to speak. Live on room service and creative snuggling for a week or so."

"When do we leave?" I said.

"Seriously," she said. "You need to watch your back."

"You, too," I said. "They knew enough to pick me up at Carla's office. They may know that I'm staying here."

"The question is why," she said.

"If I ever doubted that something is up with the Carla cases, I don't any more," I said. "Liebowitz and Bo Bergstrom and the people in Phoenix. What the hell is going on?"

Gabi brought me a Negra Modelo from the refrigerator. She had a glass of water for herself. She sat quietly for a while, pursing her lips and staring at the wall. She does that when she's thinking hard.

"Last week you were just starting a job here," she said. "Now you have three characters following you around. So what's happened between then and now?"

"I've been to Arizona asking questions about the Phoenix murders," I said. "I've been to Mexico to see Hector and Vicente."

"Right." She pushed aside the water glass and took a sip of my beer. "If I were the finest private investigator west of the Pecos, I might call that a clue."

"Hector and Vicente and I were alone in the room," I said. "Hector had henchman hanging around, like he always does. But we spoke English. Low-level guys wouldn't have any idea what we talking about."

"What if somebody was on you before that?" Gabi said. "Maybe they followed you to Hector's. They already knew that you were doing something for Carla Baca."

"How would they know that?" I said. "They would have to be watching Carla herself, or watching for anybody sniffing around the José Liebowitz and Bo Bergstrom cases. Not likely. Both those cases have been cold for months."

"The Phoenix murders, then," Gabi said.

"The only person I saw in Phoenix was your reporter friend Thomas Jenkins," I said. "He didn't strike me a murder conspirator."

Gabi laughed. "Okay, we rule him out."

"Let's see if we can rule somebody in," I said. "You have a number for the sheriff's station in West Hollywood?"

She dragged a chair next to mine and pulled her purse across the table. She took out a tiny address book and placed it in front of me. She pushed up close to supervise.

"Why three guys?" she said.

"Why not?"

"Shouldn't it be four? I mean, if they're going to use teams of two, why not all the time?"

"One called in sick?"

"Come on," she said. "Little things are important sometimes."

"You're right," I said. "Nice perfume. Chanel?"

"Walgreen's," she said. "I can excite you on the cheap."

"True," I said. I turned to the L's. In Gabi's microscopic handwriting I saw "LASD-WH." I pointed to the number and she nodded. The phone was on the table. I punched in the number and asked for Detective Jansson.

"Brinker," he said. "Clear my case for me?"

"Not yet, but I have a possible investigative lead. Can you run a plate for me?"

"Why, certainly," he said. "It's one of our most requested public services here, invading the privacy of citizens for out-of-state PI's."

"At least two teams of men tailed me today," I said. "I got the plate of one SUV just before LAPD pulled it over."

"The plot thickens," Jansson said. "What'd they stop him for?"

"Doing about seventy in front of the Police Academy in Elysian Park," I said.

"Seventy in front of a lot full of black and whites?" Jansson laughed. "Okay, so you're looking for a mental defective in an SUV with plate number what?"

I gave it to him.

"It's going to come back to a rental agency," I said. "What I'd really like is the driver's name."

Jansson said, "And my reward for this is?"

"A vanilla cone," I said. "And maybe a lead on whoever got José Liebowitz."

"Call you back," he said.

Gabi wiggled closer and put her head on my shoulder.

"If you keeping kneading my thigh like that," I said, "I'll be distracted from my important work."

"I have important work for you," she said.

Jansson called back two hours later. That was just about right for Gabi and me.

"Avis rental at LAX. Renter is James Delgado," Jansson said. "4831 Viejas, Nogales, Arizona. Proud citizen of the United States. Valid Arizona license. Age twenty-four, with a sheet going back to high school. Two narco busts for sale. One pleaded down to possession. That was good for probation. Next one got him a year at Lewis. Where's Lewis?"

"Near Gila Bend."

"Good punishment," he said. "I wouldn't even want to be *free* near Gila Bend. Let's see, two domestic beefs with a girl friend. She was hospitalized once, but she wouldn't charge. Typical. One GTA, a year in Florence."

"Bad, but not big bad," I said.

"Yep," Jansson said. "No current wants or warrants. If you're not just being paranoid, if a guy like that really is on your tail, I'm a little more interested in your conspiracy theory."

"You happen to have his driver license picture?" I asked.

"Yep. You have email where you are?"

I gave him Gabi's email address. "We need to think about this differently," I said.

"Let me know how that goes," he said.

I hung up. Gabi came back from the kitchen with two more bottles of Negra Modelo.

"Mexican beer and Chicana passion," she said. "I don't see how your life could get any better."

She gave one to me, sat on the bed, and said, "Any progress?"

"Check your email in a few minutes," I said. "Jansson's sending a picture of one of my shadows."

"He's being helpful," she said.

"He needs new information to get the Liebowitz case off the back burner," I said. "Gabi, we're thinking about this all wrong. What I've done so far seemed logical enough, but it's gone off the tracks."

"Maybe you had a bad premise," she said.

"Exactly," I said. "I've been going on the premise that this is about Carla because she's the only connection between the two murders here, and maybe that slaughter in Phoenix."

"Right," she said.

"But what if that's not it? What if Carla's just a distraction?"

"Why?" Gabi said.

"All I know is, I've got at least three hoods following me around. No immigrant smuggling outfit is going to bother. Most people smugglers don't even have resources like that."

"Drug smugglers do," she said.

"Bingo," I said. "What's the one thing a small time crook like this James Delgado might have in common with José Liebowitz? Drugs. The problem is, there's no information to put Liebowitz together with a guy like that. José was pot and some pills. Little stuff they pass around at a club on Friday night. Nobody needs low rent muscle like Delgado for the cash customers. As far as I can tell."

"I hate to be a party pooper," she said, "but if these guys are drug dealers, why wouldn't they just kill you? That's their usual response to business problems."

"Thanks for pointing that out," I said. "Check your email, okay? Then let's print a few of those pictures."

19

I called Albuquerque information for W. Elston Smythe, the lawyer who had represented Carla's father when he was beaten up by Border Patrol agents. I expected him to be retired or dead by now. But the operator had a number. A pleasant woman answered and put me through to Smythe with no questions asked.

"Mr. Brinker," Smythe said. "I haven't heard Carlos Baca's name in years and years. Who are you, sir, and why are you calling now?"

I cobbled together a story about looking for people who might want to harm Carla. I had come across the old newspaper story about her father's run-in with the Border Patrol, and wondered if there could be some connection.

"Well, I doubt that," he said.

"Why?"

"First of all, it seems terribly tenuous. It was so long ago. And the idea of someone coming after Carla makes no sense. She was just a kid. She wasn't even at the scene when her father was beaten."

"How was the case resolved?"

"No harm in telling you now, I suppose," Smythe said. "A settlement was reached. The government was actually pretty good about the whole thing. It seems the two agents who beat Carlos had a history of trouble. The Border Patrol wanted to get rid of them with as little publicity as possible. That was achieved."

"I remember thinking there was no follow-up story on the lawsuit," I said.

"Yes," he said. "The reporter who did the original story had a massive stroke a few weeks later and died. Terrible thing. A very nice woman, and not even forty years old. But with her gone and no trial in the offing, our little news story just fell through the cracks."

"What happened to the Border Patrol agents?" I said.

"Allowed to resign," Smythe said. "They moved to Florida, I'm told, and opened a check cashing service. Heard nothing about them since."

"And the settlement?" I asked.

"A lump sum in six figures," he said. "Your tax dollars at work."

"It put Carla through college and law school, I guess."

"Some of it," Smythe said. "But it was needed sooner than that. Carlos was never the same after the incident. He lost his job. He died in an automobile accident a few months later. That's why Carla's mother moved them to Tucson. Carla worshipped her father. She took his death very hard. Mrs. Baca decided they needed to get away."

"I knew Carla in high school. I never had a clue about this."

"Not surprising," the old lawyer said. "She was always good at keeping herself to herself, if you know what I mean."

"I do," I said.

20

Gabi left early to cover a story in Newport Beach. I slept until almost nine, then called Carla Baca's office. I wanted to show her Delgado's picture.

Amric took the call. "Carla is at the United States Attorney's office all morning on a client matter," he said in that wonderful accent. "Can you send the photograph electronically, Mr. Brinker?"

Gabi had taken the laptop on assignment, but she left me a disc and printed copies of the picture.

"I'll go to a copy shop and email it," I said.

"That would be excellent," Amric said. "I will see that Carla has it immediately when she returns." He gave me his email address, then said, "If you are at Miss Corona's home, the closest copy shop with customer email service is on Glencoe Avenue. Do you know where that is?"

I confessed ignorance. He gave me the address and phone number of the shop. Amric must be Carla's Radar O'Reilly, I thought. He gets what people need before they know they need it.

The phone rang as I was about to leave. Terry O'Laughlin said, "Did she try to put you on that Phoenix mess?"

"Yeah," I said.

"Me, too," he said, "Carla pays some bills for me, but I think she's gone round the bend. How can a bunch of dead Mexicans in a smuggler's safe house four-hundred miles away have anything to do with good old José and Bo?"

"I don't know," I said. "I'm like your Hollywood friends. I don't know anything yet."

"Let me give you a friendly word of advice about clients here," O'Laughlin said. "If they ask you to check for hidden cameras in their bedroom, great. If they want you to bail their cokehead kid out of jail, fine. They need somebody to drive them to their shrink or to dog sit, go for it. But they ask you to snoop around people who kill their victims four a time, that may be a little over your head." He hung up.

I left the apartment, followed Amric's directions, and found the copy shop. I had the clerk email the Delgado picture to Amric. It was nice to avoid the drive downtown. It would be even better to avoid hikes up to Camarillo or out to Riverside.

I called Bill Bergstrom and asked if he had email at the Bo's Berries office. He said yes, so I asked him to hold on. He gave me the address. I relayed it to the clerk, then waited while she sent the image again.

Bergstrom said, "I talked to the sheriff this morning. There's nothing new. He won't say so, but I really think they've moved on to other things."

"Not surprising," I said.

"No," he said. "It would take a lucky break, wouldn't it? Maybe somebody they arrest for something else will have information to trade."

"It often happens that way," I said. I could hear him tapping at his computer keyboard.

"I have the picture now," he said. There was a pause, then a sigh.

"I'm afraid not," he said. "I'm sure that I've never seen this man."

"Worth a try," I said.

"Yes," he said. "Thanks for keeping at this."

We said goodbye. I tried Sandra Liebowitz Brown's number in Riverside. Her answering machine picked up.

"It's Brinker, Mrs. Brown," I said. Maybe she was screening and would answer. No luck. I left my cell number and asked her to call.

What a case. Three phone calls exhausted my hot investigative leads. Something told me that I should be back in Arizona, learning more about the Phoenix murders. That would mean leaving Gabi, though. Life was good in that little apartment by the marina.

The copy shop sat in a cluster of stores at the outer edge of a mall parking lot. Business was slow. Nobody seemed to be coming or going. At the south end of the row, there was a twenty-four hour restaurant with a name I recognized. The chain had several locations around town and Gabi told me it wasn't bad. My watch said ten a.m. Still time for breakfast.

I strolled down the walk, checking out the display windows. A mattress store, with lots of specials this week only. A tobacconist with a big humidor in the back of the shop. Cigars always smell best to me when nobody is smoking them. There was a hobby shop with a miniature radio-controlled helicopter available in a kit for only two-hundred-eighty-nine dollars. It made me think of Richard Rawlins. I wondered if he was my best path to Carla's secrets, or if he would loyally keep them.

I never saw or heard the men behind me. A passageway separated the hobby shop and the next store down. Before I realized how distracted I had been, two pairs of hands were on my arms, twisting me into the passage. One guy stayed back while the other landed a vicious punch in my stomach and shoved me into the wall. I went down hard, gasping for breath. My head bounced off something hard. My right leg felt broken. I didn't know if I was actually unconscious or if the blows and the fall shrank my universe down to a narrow tunnel of pain. My vision was a red haze. At the edge of it, the slugger was coming toward me again. He said, "Back off, *pendejo!*" He drew his arm back and bent to hit me again. I heard a sharp pop and thought he might be trying to shoot me. But he suddenly turned around, looking toward his fellow mugger. Another pop, and the guy fell toward me. He landed on his back and hit his head hard on the walk. There was blood on his chest. Beyond him, the second man was down. Standing over him with a gun in his hand was James Delgado. He looked at his two victims and at me. His blank expression did not change. He turned and stepped quickly out of sight.

Cops sealed off the passageway. Crime scene crews crawled around it. Paramedics helped me up, looked me over, and ruled out a broken leg. They said I would recover quickly from the nasty blow to the abdomen, but I should stay alert for any wooziness or unexpected bleeding. They gave me two Tylenol tablets. They actually said, "Have a nice day, sir," as two patrol officers urged me into the back seat of a cruiser.

Jansson showed up a half-hour later. He let himself into the front seat and looked back at me.

"I assume you deny shooting those clowns," he said.

I gave him the best offended look I could manage.

"Mmm," he said. "Well, you might want to thank whoever did it. He took his gun with him. If it had been you, in your condition, we'd have found the gun pretty close by, don't you think?"

I nodded. It hurt to nod.

"Just grunt if I get something wrong here," he said. "The uniforms canvassed the area. The copy shop guy said you were in there sending some kinda picture to a person named Amric at what appears to be Carla Baca's office email. Right?"

I tried to say "Right" but managed just a wheeze. My head ached and my diaphragm still throbbed even though the attack was almost an hour ago. The palm of my right hand was scraped raw where I tried to break my fall against the gritty concrete.

"So I'm guessing it was the picture of James Delgado that I got for you."

"Right."

"You think these guys tried to kill you or just ruin your day?"

"Rough me up." I took a breath, gingergly, and said, "The guy working on me told me to back off. It felt more like a warning than attempted murder."

"That's what I think. And like I said, we didn't find any guns on them, either. Indicates a lack of homicidal purpose. You seen them before? Anything about them I should know?"

"No. One of them said *pendejo* instead of asshole, and it sounded like pretty authentic Spanish."

"Oh, they were authentic, all right," Jansson said. "Lotta Latinos involved in your life. Hispanic tails yesterday. These dead creeps are from East L.A. Both of them have jackets for narcotics, extortion, assault. I called a friend of mine, gang guy on LAPD. We'll see if he can help me."

I massaged my temples. I wished for Gabi.

Jansson said, "Maybe they didn't have to tail you. Maybe somebody told them you were here."

"I don't think so," I said.

"Who knew you were here?"

"Just Amric at Carla's office," I said. "Anybody he told."

"Amric what?" Jansson said.

"I don't know his full name. That's a stretch, though. He's Carla's assistant. Why would he send anybody after me?"

"A fair question," Jansson said, "but not exactly an answer. How come you're not packing, when you know guys are after you?"

I shook my head. "No California license."

He gave me an are-you-kidding-me look. "You might want to consider a violation on that one," he said. "I'll never tell."

"I can use you for a reference?"

"Sure. So, Brinker, you got one bunch of hoods tailing you, that bunch or somebody else beating the shit out of you, and James Delgado just happens to show up and blow two of them away. You're in some kind of weird position, son."

"Stuck in the middle with you," I said.

"He faded away afterwards, apparently," Jansson said. "Nobody actually saw the shooting. He could just step around the shops here and hop into a car, or go through the mall and get his car on the other side."

"He was lucky nobody came down the front sidewalk," I said.

Jansson laughed. "No, the guy who didn't come down the walk was the lucky one. You're right, though. This character gets pinched for speeding past the Police Academy, but when he decides to plug two *hermanos*, there's not a cop around. Or even a witness."

"Except me," I said.

"I was wondering about that," he said. "The guy's a two-bit hood. He shoots to kill. When he caught up to you, he could have just as easily have taken you out, too. What's that about? He been won over by your dashing personality, Brinker?"

"Like you told me once," I said, "that would be a first."

21

Jansson let me go. I limped to my car and drove slowly back to Gabi's apartment. There was one vacant parking space. I squeezed in between a metallic blue BMW sedan and a gleaming black Chevy Trail Blazer. Terry O'Laughlin got out of the Blazer. When he saw my face, he laughed.

"How's your day so far?" he said.

"Let's talk later, O'Laughlin," I said.

"Now's the perfect time," he said. He blocked my way, his big shoulders filling the narrow space between my car and the BMW.

"Make it fast," I said.

"Sure," he said. "I was going to tell you that you're over your head here. The way you look, maybe you know that already."

"You told me already," I said.

"Carla chews up guys like us and spits us out," he said. "Bats those big dark eyes and sings her little justice-for-the-downtrodden song. You think you can hold her interest?"

"Look," I said. "I'm not working for love. I'm an investigator and Carla's paying me to investigate. The job will go where it goes. When it's done, I go home."

"Or maybe come right here," he said, tilting his head toward Gabi's apartment building.

"The point is, I'm not after Carla. I don't care if I see her again after I finish this job. You're the one who sounds hung up on her."

He backed up to let me pass.

"Remember what I told you," he said.

"One thing, O'Laughlin," I said. "I don't want people hanging around here. Gabriela Corona isn't part of this."

"My God, you're dense," he said. "A couple of gangbangers jump you the first time you walk by an alley. It took me about two minutes to find out where you'd be right now. How long do you think you or your girl friend would last if somebody was seriously after you?"

"How did you know who attacked me?" I said.

O'Laughlin smiled and said, "When you know what you're doing, even the big city is a small world."

He climbed back into the Blazer and laughed. "You know what the old gubernator used to say. *Hasta la vista*, baby."

Gabi didn't like whiskey, but she kept a bottle of Makers Mark for me. I poured an inch into the fattest glass I could find. I took it out to the balcony. My watch said almost one o'clock. The marine layer of haze hung on, making the mid-July day feel more like spring or early summer. The breeze was off the ocean, pushing smoke from the La Habra Heights fire inland. Southern Californians talk about May Gray and June Gloom. I could use Maigret on this case, I thought. Gloom I already have.

I had assumed that James Delgado was part of a tag team that followed me from Carla's office to Dodger Stadium. That was still possible. The guys who jumped me could have been part of some other team. But if so, why had I attracted two groups of men following me around Los Angeles? If someone meant me harm, why not just shoot me in that shopping center passageway?

Then there was the other possibility. What if the muggers were part of the team that picked me up downtown, and James Delgado was watching *them*?

I looked in Gabi's medicine cabinet and found a bottle of Vicodin. A little sticker said, "Do not take with alcohol." Taking a Vicodin with another glass of Makers seemed like a fine idea, but I still had some sense left. I looked at the rest of the label. The prescription had been filled two years ago. Gabi was helping me with a case about that time. That's when she got a broken wrist and a banged up face for her trouble. What a guy, Brinker. Drag her into one mess after another. Sit in her apartment drinking her booze and almost swiping her drugs. I closed the cabinet and went back to the living room.

CNN had an update from the La Habra Heights fires. Then they showed grainy black-and-white footage of a nearby canyon where fire crews from the old California Youth Authority got caught by flames when a gust of wind ignited a smoldering hillside. It happened in 1958, the announcer said. Four kids died, teenagers in custody trying to earn a little time off their sentences by fighting fires.

My cell rang. It was Jansson.

"We found your late buddies' car in the mall parking lot," he said. "It kinda stood out. Whittier Boulevard special. Lowrider fifty-eight Impala."

"You're kidding," I said. "Their getaway car was more than fifty years old?"

"Probably runs better than anything I could take out of the motor pool," Jansson said. "Pretty cool looking, too. Pristine paint, waxed to the max. They'll use it in the funerals. Anyway, the registration matches one of our unfortunate perps, Victor Molina. Mean anything?"

"Nothing."

"I figured. Local hires. An upstanding P.I. from Tucson would have no reason to recognize them."

"Nobody would send a tail in a lowrider," I said. "Like you say, it stands out."

"I never promised you brilliant crooks," he said. "Besides, did you notice them before they stomped on you?"

"There is that," I said.

"L.A. County's forty-seven percent Hispanic," he said. "Some parts of this county have more lowriders than Camrys."

"I'll be more alert next time," I said.

"I just hung up," Jansson said. "This is not me talking to you. Get a goddam gun."

"Very soon," I said.

Gabi got home at five-thirty.

"Two-and-a-half hours from Newport," she said, coming in the door, fiddling with keys and purse, not seeing me yet. "I need a chauffeur. You think if I flirted with Richard Rawlins, he'd fly me around in his helicopter?"

"You could try," I said, "but his heart belongs to Carla."

She turned around and got her first look at me. Scraped forehead and hand. Swollen leg up on the coffee table. The effect of several Makers Marks on my face.

"What happened?" she said.

"A little disagreement with some local talent," I said.

Gabi laughed and tried the old joke. "What does the other guy look like?"

"Two guys," I said. "They look dead."

"Jesus," she said. "You're serious, aren't you?" She almost ran to the sofa and sat beside me. She put an arm around my shoulder and pressed her face against my chest.

"You killed two guys?" she said. Gabi was tough and steady in a clutch, but this time her voice caught. She held me tight. I told her what happened.

"A couple of *vatos* from East L.A.," I said. "Hired help. The question is who sent them."

Gabi sat up and looked me over. "Wow," she said. "I had this nice little pitch all prepared, about how you could move over here and we could live together in tranquility."

"Don't rule it out," I said. "But tomorrow, I'm going home. I need my gun. I'll get my own car and drive back here. Maybe throw off some of these guys who find me so interesting."

"When are you coming back?"

"As soon as I can. I want to see if Al can get anything on the cop grapevine about Phoenix. If there's something worth checking, I'll stay and do that. Otherwise, L.A. seems to be where the action is."

"I told you to watch your back," she said.

"I didn't do that. Stupid. Careless."

Gabi stood up and went to the kitchen. She found an open bottle of red wine and poured a glass. She turned around and looked hard at me.

"Wait a minute," she said. "This guy Delgado shows up, kills two men, and doesn't hurt you?"

"That's right. Just turned around and faded into the mall."

"But you saw him do it. Why would he leave a witness?"

"No good reason," I said. "Fits perfectly with this case. Two young guys get murdered. No reason. A bunch of people in Phoenix get slaughtered. No reason. Carla hires me but holds out on information I need. Think I should have another drink?"

"No reason why not," Gabi said. "You aren't going anywhere tonight."

22

Southwest got me to Tucson at nine a.m. I ransomed my car from the airport lot and drove to the post office. I filled out the form to have my mail forwarded to Gabi's address. At home, I found three days worth in the streetside box. The house was hot and stuffy. The burglar alarm light glowed steadily, undisturbed, beeping only when I unlocked the back door.

I spent an hour reading the Arizona newspapers online, looking for new scraps about the Phoenix murders. The Tucson daily had nothing new. The Phoenix paper stuck with the theme of a vaguely defined war among people-smuggling gangs. A reporter even flew to Mexico City to interview the federal Attorney General. He knew about the smuggling problem, but not about the "particular tragedy," as he called it. The Phoenix alternative weekly reported that Maricopa County's showboat sheriff was trying to get some jurisdiction on the murders, even though they happened in city police territory.

Al Avila arrived at eleven o'clock. Full dress uniform with necktie. Captain's insignia looked good on the tunic shoulders.

"Best dressed cop in Tucson," I said.

"I've been ordered to attend the Chamber of Commerce luncheon," he said. "I wanted to show up with SWAT gear, in case the speeches go too long. The chief said no."

We traded news of Anna and Gabi. Al and Anna's daughters, Anita and Alicia, couldn't wait to get to summer camp at Flagstaff. Al had moved his Saturday run up to five a.m. Every day now topped one-hundred-five degrees.

"I've got one thing for you from Phoenix," Al said. He pulled a manila envelope from his briefcase. "Phoenix PD is circulating this very quietly. No publicity. You can use it, but don't give it to Carla."

"Okay," I said.

He took a photograph from the envelope and passed it to me. It was a surveillance shot from the Homeland Security office in El Paso. The subject was a male Hispanic, short with a solid build, good haircut, and a nice looking Hawaiian shirt.

"Eduardo Salvador," Al said. "Born in Denver and has a home there. But he spends a lot of time in border towns. He's been observed hanging around with known drug and immigrant smugglers. Never been arrested in Arizona, but he got popped for a couple of assault charges in California. Probation both times. His name surfaces in an investigation every year or so, but nothing outstanding on him now."

"What does he have to do with Phoenix?"

"Nothing beats a smart cop on the street," Al said. "Some patrol officer was going through a book of smuggling suspects, just to see if anything rang a bell. He said he's seen this guy at a couple of fast food joints near the crime scene. The guy stood out because he was a better dressed than the usual customers there. Big old gold Rolex on his wrist and a Cadillac Escalade outside."

"Subtle," I said.

"Vanity catches a lot of bad guys. Anyway, this smart young cop starts eating three meals a day at the fast food places. That kid'll make detective if Mr. Salvador reappears."

"And he hasn't, since the murders," I said.

"Not yet," Al said. "Phoenix asked Denver to roll by the Salvador house up there. Everything looks cool, but there's no sign of the man himself. Now it's getting interesting, so a Denver detective asks around the neighborhood. The guy lives alone. Very quiet. Always pleasant. Buys Girl Scout cookies. Has a yard service come in weekly, so even if he's away, the place looks good. Grass cut in the summer, leaves raked in the fall, walk shoveled in the winter. But Salvador hasn't been seen up there for three weeks."

"Timing is just right," I said.

"So I thought you should have this," Al said. "If you cross paths with this guy, it's probably no accident. Given his known associates, he could have something to do with the guys who jumped you."

He looked at his watch and stood.

"Can't be late," he said.

"You ever hear of James Delgado from Nogales?" I asked as we walked to the door.

"Nope. Bad guy or good guy?"

"Bad."

"You know Bill Orozco on Nogales PD?"

"Sounds familiar," I said. "He was there when we were on the Patrol, I think."

"That's the guy. He's still there. Keeps track of the local lowlife. Give him a call."

Orozco, on the phone, said, "James Delgado? Oh, yeah. Good old Jimmy D."

"Close personal friend?" I said.

He laughed. "More like a frequent guest here. Not that many arrests, actually, but we always seem to have questions for him regarding pharmaceutical transactions."

"Who does he work for?" I asked.

"Freelance," Orozco said. "It's mostly freelance on this side of the fence. In Mexico, all the serious hoods are in gangs. A gang is like a blood relation over there. Things are lots worse than when you and Al worked the border. On our side, though, we have lots of young guys like Jimmy D, hanging out, picking up any jobs that come along."

"Is he into immigrant smuggling?"

"Hmm, sounds a little outside his usual portfolio. Jimmy D mostly moves drugs on the street around here. His stay in the pen was for a car theft up in Tucson, I think."

"You see him as a hitter?"

"Well, that would be a major escalation for him," Orozco said. "We got the bulletin from the L.A. sheriff, so I know what you're talking about. He was never that rough around here. We never even got him with a weapon."

"And nothing suspicious along the border?"

"We have pictures of him crossing, going and coming at the pedestrian Port of Entry. But we can't keep track of every small time crook who walks into Mexico. He could be going to get laid, or drinking cheap beer, or catching a bus for the beach at Guaymas, for all I know."

"Seen him lately?" I asked.

"Nobody's mentioned him for a while," I said. "We went by his place when L.A. called us, but he's not around. Lives with his mother, you believe that? She said he's a good boy now, but she hasn't seen him for two weeks."

Longer than he had been watching me, but about right for the Phoenix job, I thought. If only I had a way to connect him with it.

"How about Eduardo Salvador?" I said.

"I know the name," Orozco said. "Nothing on him. Guilt by association, maybe. He's been seen with some unpleasant characters here in Nogales and other places."

"No buzz down there on the Phoenix murders?"

"We see a lot of nervous people with gallon water jugs hanging around the Mexican side of the fence," he said. "All those poor devils know about the Phoenix thing, but they're still looking for *coyotes*. They're coming over, murders or not."

23

Something was happening at the Gila River Indian reservation as I sped up I-10 to Phoenix.

Three helicopters moved in slow circles above an undeveloped area west of the freeway. It wasn't unusual to see military choppers in the area since the September 11 attacks, but these were television crews. They flew JetRangers and Aerostars with bright station logos on their sides.

The aerial cluster must have looked ominous to people on the ground. Two Phoenix TV helicopters had collided over a city park only months before. They were following a trivial police pursuit, some jerk who had stolen a pickup truck. Two pilots and two photographers died for a useless story that wouldn't have deserved ten seconds on the news. Today, some poor devil died out there in the desert, I figured, and the so-called news teams swarmed over the story. Meanwhile, gamblers and golfers raced down the off ramp to the reservation casino and resort.

Thomas Jenkins met me at Arizona State University in Tempe. He was sitting in the meager shade of a dehydrated tree on the lawn outside Grady Gammage. ASU claims that it was the last building designed by Frank Lloyd Wright. It's a distinctive round auditorium with stone sections scalloped at the top to look like stage curtains. They use it for big campus functions and traveling Broadway shows.

"Why here?" I said.

"Serious donation announcement," he said. "They got five-hundred-million dollars from a 31-year-old graduate who runs a hedge fund. Half the movers and shakers in Phoenix were here this morning. Does your car have air?"

"Sure," I said.

"Mine doesn't work," he said. "Let's sit in yours."

We climbed in and I restarted the engine. The air conditioning kicked right in. I could feel Al Gore scowling. Jenkins used a once-white handkerchief to wipe his brow.

"The first settlers here must not have arrived in July," he said.

I had a couple of plastic water bottles in the back seat. I gave him one. He downed half of it.

"Much better," he said. "I came to this thing because the police chief was here. All the city poo-bahs showed up. The thing is, the chief has stopped making statements. He doesn't return his calls. The department flack calls me back and says there's no new comment. Chief Kalven's usually pretty chatty, even on big cases. Now there's a freeze on information."

"Did you get to the chief?"

"Yeah. I cornered him after the ceremony. He didn't dodge me, I'll give him that. He said 'off the record?' I said okay. He told me that the case is getting more complicated than anyone thought. Bottom line is, nobody will talk publicly for a while."

"Complicated," I said. "The feds are coming in, I'll bet. They're telling him, we have bigger issues involved than a few local homicides."

"That's my guess," Jenkins said. "I asked him about other agencies. He just smiled and ended the conversation."

He was about to tell me something else when his cell phone rang. He answered with his name, listened for a moment, then said, "Thanks. I'm on the way."

"What's up?" I asked.

"Four bodies found on the reservation," he said. "Gunshot wounds."

"How about if I drive?" I said. "I know right where they are."

The television news helicopters still hovered over the crime scene. Now Sheriff Showboat had one of his choppers there, too. Hope springs eternal. Jenkins flashed his press pass for the tribal police officer guarding the perimeter. The man waved us through without a word. He didn't ask about me. He must have figured that journalists have chauffeurs.

The second checkpoint was tougher. Tribal police, Border Patrol agents, uniformed Arizona Department of Public Safety officers, and Anglos with white shirts and shoulder holsters held everyone back. We were fifty yards from the bodies. The usual crew of crime scene specialists and coroner's functionaries moved about.

Jenkins pointed at a thin man with brown hair who was watching from twenty feet away. Another man stood with him, occasionally turning to say something.

"That's Kalven, the skinny one," Jenkins said. "I think the other guy is FBI."

"If Kalven is here, this is tied up with the immigrant murders," I said. "The res is out of his jurisdiction. I can tell you what he's thinking. He's thinking the Feebies are going to use this to take over his case."

Kalven turned and walked toward the reporters. Jenkins yelled, "Chief!" but Kalven just held up his hands and said, "No comment yet." His face had reddened. It could have been the sun, but I bet on anger.

As he walked by, I said, "Chief, I might have a name for one of those people."

He stopped and came up close to me.

"Who are you?" he said.

"My name's Brinker," I said. "I'm a private investigator from Tucson."

"How did you get in here?"

"Resourcefulness," I said.

"Save the wisecracks, pal," he said. "What's the name?"

The reporters were moving in to listen. I leaned in and said as quietly as possible, "Lourdes Ortega."

Kalven looked back to the crime scene. He turned and sized up the gathering reporters. He took a business card from his shirt pocket and scribbled something on it. He handed it to me and walked away. A young uniformed officer opened the back door of a big Ford sedan. Kalven got in. The officer got behind the wheel. The car kicked up an enormous dust cloud as it sped toward the freeway.

I looked at the card. The police chief had written, "Oaxaca, 3 p.m." When I looked up, Jenkins was staring at me.

"You owe me," he said.

"I do," I said.

"Who the hell is Lourdes Ortega?"

"A woman who might have been in the group of illegals," I said.

Jenkins thought about that. He said, "The chief's reaction didn't tell us much."

"He may have more to tell," I said. "Or maybe he just wants to pump me for information. Where are you going to be at, say, four o'clock?"

He held up his cell phone.

"Probably here," he said. "I know one of the crime scene guys. I might be able to get something from him. You go ahead. I'll hitch a ride with one of the other reporters. "

"I'll call you if I get anything you can use," I said.

"Call me no matter what," he said. "You owe me."

24

Oaxaca was a Mexican restaurant on West Van Buren, near many of the state government buildings. Usually business boomed, but three o'clock was right between the lunch crowd and before-dinner margarita rush. I parked in the lot next door. The chief's driver sat in the entrance lobby, sipping a soda. He cocked his head toward the bar. They called it a cantina. It was dark, cool, and quiet, the kind of little bar you found all over Arizona before hospitality consultants took over. Kalven sat by himself at a small table near the back. He had a bottle of Corona and some chips and salsa on the table.

"Want something?" he said as I sat down.

"Beer looks terrific," I said. "Anything cold."

He caught the bartender's eye and ordered my beer. The woman brought it, then returned to the other end of the bar and made herself busy, polishing glasses.

"Talk to me," Kalven said. "Lourdes Ortega."

"She there?" I asked.

"No female was there. All males. Youngish. No IDs. Their clothes were too good to be illegal immigrants, so we're thinking they were smugglers. *Coyotes.*"

"How did you put them together with the murders?"

"How do you know we did?" he asked.

"Why would you be there otherwise?" I said. "Why would anyone from Phoenix PD be on the res, let alone the chief?"

Kalven took a long drink of his beer. He put the glass down softly, looked at me, and said, "Okay."

I dipped a chip in the salsa. Pretty good. Not too much onion, with a nice mix of tomato, cilantro, and chili flavors. I drank some beer.

"How long were the bodies there?" I said.

"The coroner gave me a ballpark time. Less than three weeks, but not by much. He needs to get them back to his place to narrow it down. You know how it is when they're out in the desert for a while."

"So that would be about perfect for timing, wouldn't it?" I said.

Kalven nodded and said, "Your turn. Who is Lourdes Ortega, and what does she have to with that murder house?"

"She's a woman from Guaymas who was planning to come up here," I said. "No documents. I have reason to believe that she was coming through Phoenix, en route to L.A."

"What do you mean, reason to believe?" he said.

"Information provided to someone I know," I said.

"Don't get cute," Kalven said. "I've got a multiple murder investigation here, and jack shit for evidence. The Bureau is making noises about jurisdiction because these latest bodies were on the res and may be tied to illegal immigration. Our dipshit sheriff is trying to butt in, get some TV face time. I've got pretty low tolerance for anyone who withholds relevant information."

"I gave you the information I have," I said. "Where I got it isn't relevant to your investigation."

"That's not something you get to decide," he said.

I sat back and took another drink, watching him over the glass.

"Okay, okay," he said. "Riding over here, I made a call to the Tucson police chief. We're old pals. He was just coming out of a luncheon somewhere. I asked about you, and he handed the phone to a Captain Avila, who was with him."

I smiled.

"Yeah, he vouched for you," Kalven said. "So I'll cut you a little slack today. I'll even buy your beer. What else can you tell me about Lourdes Ortega?"

"She was coming up with her husband and child," I said. "I don't know exactly when. I don't know the husband's name or how old the baby is. The thing that worried me was that milk carton at the murder house."

Kalven jumped on that. "How did you know about a milk carton?"

"I must have read it in the news," I said.

"No, you didn't," he said. "We held that back. A couple of reporters got it, probably from some chatty uniform. But we asked them to sit on it and they did. They gave us their usual First Amendment huffing and puffing, even though that's all crap and they know it. They can withhold anything they want if they choose to be decent citizens."

"Hmm," I said.

"And you were standing with Tom Jenkins out there in the desert," he said. "That's why I stopped to talk you in the first place. I need to give Tom a little reminder about mutual cooperation."

"Don't blame him," I said. "If there's a kid angle in this, it would get out eventually."

He sighed and said, "Yeah." He drank the last of his beer. He took a roll of breath mints from his shirt pocket. He offered me one. We both sat there, sucking on our mints.

"Here's something maybe you don't know," he said. "You have a deal with Jenkins?"

"A little one," I said.

"Well, you tell him if he passes this on, I'll personally shoot out the headlight on his jalopy and have him ticketed every time he drives after dark. What he makes at the AP, I can bankrupt him in about a week."

"Okay," I said.

"Three of the four victims in that house had identification," he said. "Mexican ID card, voter card, driver license from Sonora or one of the other states. Everybody except one male, age late twenties. All the others had ID. No reason not to. So what happened to it?"

"Whoever killed him took it because his name would give something away," I said.

"Why would it matter? We know who everyone else was. It hasn't helped us a bit, except to notify families."

"Because," I said, "if you had his name and knew where he lived, you could ask questions there. And you might find out that he came north with a woman and a baby. But that would make him a victim, not a smuggler."

Kalven was scratching at the label of the Corona bottle.

"I liked it when these had paper labels," he said. "If they kept the bottles in ice water, you could peel off the labels. I had a collection of Mexican beer labels once."

"A lot of Mexicans are named Ortega," I said. "Even in Guaymas, there must be hundreds."

Kalven smiled. "There's a guy on the State Judicial Police in Sonora. He was up here for one of those stupid international conferences we have. I got him Diamondback tickets one night."

"His turn to do you a favor," I said.

"I'll say. It was interleague week. The Yankees were in town. A kid from Hermosillo drove in the winning run for the D'backs. Believe me, this guy will do anything for me."

"Reel him in," I said.

The police chief took out another business card and wrote some numbers on the back.

"Private office line, home, and cell," he said. "I'm taking a flier on you, Brinker. I want to know what you know, just as soon as you know it."

"This Ortega thing could really move the case," I said.

"Jesus," he said. "I hope something does."

Phoenix is two hours closer than Tucson to L.A. I missed Gabi. I felt an ache that had nothing to do with being beaten up. I could drive home, pack some things, then drive for eight more hours to see her. Or I could leave Phoenix right now and be with her in six hours. From the parking lot of Oaxaca, I called her cell.

"What are you doing right now?" I said.

"There's a original opening line," she said. "I'm in Chatsworth. The porn performers are threatening to go on strike. Our regular porn industry reporters are on vacation, and I got the assignment. If you were thinking of phone sex, I'm in a great position, so to speak."

"This isn't one of those reporter involvement features, is it?"

"No, no, no," she said. "Journalistic detachment on this one, for sure."

"I'm in Phoenix. If I hit the road right now, I could be at the marina by eleven. Midnight for sure. That okay?"

"I'll get out my romantic light supper cookbook," she said. "Maybe I can get a few dessert ideas here in Porn Valley."

"I've got some screwy thoughts about this case. I need to see Carla again, and I need your brain."

Gabi said, "I'm sorry, but I don't offer the brain separately. You have to take the entire woman and work your way up."

"You're spending too much time in the valley," I said.

25

I drove toward the sun through the grim bleached desert along I-10. The speed limit signs say seventy-five. Arizonans consider that a minimum. I crossed the Colorado River. The California agriculture inspection station was closed, so freeway traffic sped past it. I stopped for gas and a drive-thru burger in Blythe.

I called Jenkins in Phoenix. I told him what Kalven had and mentioned the headlight embargo on publication. Jenkins laughed and said he'd play along.

The sun was low and still bright. At Palm Springs, I raised the window visor and pressed on into the twilight. As I sped down the hill at Redlands, the sky darkened and traffic thickened. Welcome to exurban Los Angeles. I saw the sign for Riverside and wondered why Sandra Liebowitz Brown, who was so eager for progress, had not called me back.

Gabi's L.A. oldies station was still too far away. It hissed and crackled. I put in a Roy Orbison CD. The traffic picked up speed west of San Bernardino so I skipped the tracks to something upbeat. "I Drove All Night." The good die too soon, Roy. You'd still be making great music today. I backed up to the fabulous "Crying" duet with k.d. lang. I remembered watching her perform it alone on a tribute show after Orbison died. She almost broke down singing it. I almost broke down watching. Which was better television, k.d. that night or Kirk Gibson hitting the home run off Dennis Eckersley in the World Series?

Stream of consciousness on the freeway. Anything to keep my mind off four bodies in a broiling Phoenix house, and four more in the desert, and Lourdes Ortega and her child. They were probably dead somewhere else. But maybe not. Please, God, maybe not.

You can drive I-10 almost from the Atlantic at Jacksonville to within a few blocks of the Pacific at Santa Monica. I cut off at Lincoln Avenue and zigged along the surface streets to the marina. I called Gabi from five minutes away. She was waiting at her open door with a Pilsner Urquell in one hand and a bath towel over her arm.

"Have a drink. Take a shower," she said. "Then we'll see what you feel like." She pulled me in for a kiss. I considered staying right there for a week or so. She stepped back and said, "Shower. Definitely."

I drank half the beer while the shower water warmed up. The heat and steam cleansed me of the desert crime scene dust and soothed the aches from the long drive. I kept clean clothes in Gabi's bedroom. I dressed and went outside. The little balcony barely had room for our two chairs.

"How'd it go with the pornographers?" I said.

"Oh, boy," she said. "I thought I was pretty sophisticated, covering news here in the big city. But there are some things a nice Catholic girl from Tucson just isn't ready for. I talked with this one actress. Her job today was having sex with three guys in one scene. I asked her why she and the others are going to strike. You know what she said, perfectly straight faced? For better working conditions."

"Sad," I said.

"I wrote the story mostly about the negotiations," Gabi said. "I had some good interviews with a couple of stars and three producers. My editor wanted more on-the-set stuff. Lots of careful descriptions of moaning and writhing. I wrote that it looked like Cirque du Soleil for degenerates, but they cut that."

"I'd have made that the headline," I said.

She gestured toward the marina. "You know," she said, "just a few miles from here, a really short distance from the coast, southern California is a desert. We pipe in water, but basically we're faking it."

"I lost your train of thought there," I said. "Porn to the desert."

"I think I'm faking it, Brink. Who needs the stories I'm writing? Some days I feel like I'd be better off selling shoes."

We sat for a few minutes, listening to the breeze tug on sail riggings and rock the boats against their bumpers.

"The dirty movie producers are worried about the Internet ruining their business model," Gabi said. "So are my bosses. Which will last longer, do you think? Newspapers or porn?"

"Whichever one adapts better," I said. "That's what all businesses have to do now. Hector says even the crooks in Mexico have to change."

Gabi took my hand and raised it to her lips and kissed it, then rested her cheek against it.

What happened in Phoenix?" she said.

"Four guys found on the Gila River reservation, shot to death," I said. "The Phoenix police chief told me that everyone believes the victims were involved with the murders at that house."

"They were the smugglers?"

"Or illegal immigrants. Or part of a group that challenged the smugglers and lost. That's the thing about this. We have no idea who's doing what. It's like when I was beaten up. Who did the beating? Who wanted me tailed? Where the hell did James Delgado come from?"

Gabi sat silently in thinking mode, pursing her lips, looking out over the boat slips. The breeze eased. I heard faint sounds of laughter from the patios of restaurants on Admiralty Way. Planes from LAX rose silently over the ocean, their trajectories purposeful, their wingtip lights blinking. From this perspective, they looked tiny and slow.

"How about this?" Gabi said. "The bad guys, whoever they are, killed everyone except the woman and her baby. That was too brutal even for a bunch of amoral thugs."

"The tender murderer," I said.

"I know," she said. "What is that? Browning? In real life, it sounds ridiculous. It isn't logical. But how are you doing with logic?"

"Not getting far," I said.

"It's a crazy guess, but if it's right," Gabi said, "that woman and baby are still alive. It would make no sense to take them somewhere else and kill them."

"We don't know for sure that any woman and child were there."

"Somebody had milk. It had to be a child, don't you think? No *coyote* would have taken breakfast orders. He would have just grabbed so many sandwiches and so many coffees. Then if he had some unexpected twitch of decency, he might have said, oh, I should get milk for the kid. And that woman who wrote to Carla was coming through Phoenix with a child."

"He wouldn't bother with food if all those people were about to be murdered," I said.

"Of course not."

"Carla again," I said. "How much of this bounces back to Carla?"

"Two dead clients plus, what was the woman's name? Lourdes?"

"Lourdes Ortega."

"Two dead clients plus Lourdes Ortega, who just happened to write to a lawyer who had two clients murdered recently," Gabi said. "Brink, this all comes back to Carla."

26

Carla Baca invaded enemy territory. She stood at a ballroom lectern in the Ritz-Carlton Laguna Niguel, telling the wealthy members of the Orange County International Exchange Council why immigration was good for them.

"It's strange," she had said when I called her that morning. "Orange County isn't the conservative monolith it used to be. But the part with money still is. And they're torn on immigration. Legal immigration is wonderful. It made America great, and all that. Illegal immigration is bad. But half of them have undocumented immigrants working for them in their homes and their businesses."

"How do you talk to them?" I asked.

"Would you like to see?" she said. "Rich is flying me down there. You can come along."

"Okay," I said. "Coat and tie?"

"Always nice," she said. "Meet us at the Santa Monica Airport. Say 10:30." She gave me directions to the spot where Rawlins kept his helicopter.

By 10:45 we were in the air, headed southeast. Carla sat up front with Rawlins. I took one of the two rear seats. We didn't talk much. Carla looked over her speech. Rawlins peered warily through the haze. We raced down the I-5, leaving its strangled traffic behind. I thought we would pass over Disneyland, but Rawlins flew well north of it.

"Nothing under three-thousand feet, closer than three miles to a big amusement park," he said. "It's a 9/11 restriction. Easier to go around than to climb that high."

We continued east, staying under the John Wayne Airport traffic. At the closed El Toro Marine Corps Air Station, Rawlins turned due south and made for the coast at Laguna.

"Where do you land down there?" I said.

I couldn't see his smile but I heard it in his voice.

"It helps to be visiting the big shots," he said. "Watch."

To our left, construction boomed south of the hotel complex. Great fake palazzos were going up above the beach, built on sharply cut earthen ledges reinforced with concrete retaining walls and mesembraynthemum. Apparently California has enough pristine coastline, but not enough ostentatious houses.

A small grassy park lay just north of the hotel. It provided public access to the ocean. The park ran from the roadway at a steep incline down to the beach paths, broken by a wide and level middle section. I saw two cop cars there with lights flashing. Rawlins hovered over the space between the cruisers and put the chopper down softly on the grass. When the engine shut down and the rotors came to rest, an Orange County sheriff's deputy walked up to the door on Carla's side. Terry O'Laughlin stood next to him. He did not look happy to see me in the helicopter.

Carla pushed the door open. The deputy offered his hand to help her down.

"Miss Baca," he said, "I hope you don't mind riding a luggage cart over to the hotel. It's just a couple of minutes."

Carla unavoidably showed a little thigh as she stepped down. She beamed her best smile and said, "Can I ride up front with you?"

"Well, sure, ma'am," the young Latino deputy said. He blushed. Carla Baca wins another heart.

Rawlins and I took a side seat on the hotel's cart. O'Laughlin took the other side, and away we all went. The second deputy stayed behind to guard the helicopter. I wondered if he was moonlighting or on the county clock.

Inside, the Council chairman made a big fuss of welcoming Carla. He introduced her to the members who gathered round and led her to the head table. The crowd was California Club, a lot dressy and just a little snazzy. Men wore mostly conservative tailored suits, but a few went with pastel sport jackets. Women favored the bright summer frocks of ladies who lunch. Carla was curvy but not immodest in a dark blue suit, the skirt cut just above her knees, a designer scarf of bright colors at her neck. It was businesslike for the men and unthreatening to the women. I wondered if she had a consultant for such things or if they came naturally to beautiful people.

Rawlins and I found two places at a table near the back. O'Laughlin went to the front of the room and stood next to a side door. He had a good view of the podium and anyone who entered late. He kept scanning the room and smiling. Playing Secret Service agent, I thought. All he needed was a telltale pin in his lapel. His suit jacket was unbuttoned. Every so often, he reached inside and touched the area below his left armpit, just in case somebody failed to get the message.

Lunch was a small seafood salad followed by lamb chops or a grilled chicken breast. They probably had vegetarian and vegan versions, too. This group got the Ritz-Carlton's good china. Wine was served with the chops and chicken, but not too much. As waiters brought dessert and coffee, the Council chairman made a few housekeeping remarks and introductions. He reminded everyone that the Vice President of the United States would be September's speaker.

"This afternoon," he said, "our talk will turn, as it often does in Southern California, to immigration. Our guest is one of this area's best known immigration lawyers." He spoke her job title with the tone he might have used for a very good gardener or mechanic. He described her education, rich enough even for this gang, and her practice history.

Carla rose to polite applause. She acknowledged the head table and expressed her pleasure at being invited.

"*Y ahora*," she said, "*¿cuántos hablan español?*"

About thirty hands rose. The Spanish speakers seemed mixed evenly between Latinos and Anglos. I figured the crowd for two-hundred people.

Then Carla said something in a language I didn't recognize. I looked at Rawlins. He leaned over, close to me.

"Same question in Vietnamese," he whispered. "She can't speak it, but she has a professor friend at USC. He teaches her a phrase or two for events like this."

Maybe four hands were up. All four people looked as though they learned their Vietnamese at home.

Carla bestowed her megawatt smile and said, "To those who raised their hands, welcome to the new world. You're already part of it. To those who didn't, you will be soon, ready or not."

The hand raisers grinned, although a little guiltily, like the smart kids at Tucson High when graded exams were handed back. The rest of the crowd looked undecided and uncomfortable. You could almost hear them thinking, is she going be a nice grateful little Mexican girl or some radical Aztlan bitch?

"Don't fear this change," Carla said. "It's here, and it's growing, no matter what we want. The secret for us is to manage this change in a way that serves our society, and serves the people who want to come here legally, play by the rules, and work hard to grab their share of the American dream."

That drew applause. Nobody stood up and roared approval, but Carla had scored. They didn't expect that from her. These folks liked others to play by the rules.

Rawlins leaned over to me again and said, "The 'we' and 'us' stuff really works well. Isn't she beautiful?"

And she was, smiling modestly but basking in the warmth until the last hands clapped. Then she moved a little closer to the microphone and spoke softly.

"Now, I'm an immigration lawyer. I help people become legal residents and citizens of our United States of America. I'll bet that everyone in this room approves of that wonderful inclusive process established by our law." Heads nodded in agreement.

"But I won't kid you. You read the newspapers. You watch television. You know that another part of my job is fighting for people who want to be residents here, often when our government opposes their efforts. And when I do that, I'm sure that some of you consider me the bad guy." She said that brightly with a self-effacing smile. She earned a few polite chuckles.

"And," she said, "you may consider those clients of mine to be threats to our economy or even to our national security."

Now she was treading right at the dangerous edge of this congregation's faith. The viscosity of the room's atmosphere changed, despite the silent perfection of the Ritz-Carlton's air conditioners. Nobody coughed. No coffee cups rattled on saucers. There was not a whisper of conversation. Carla had all eyes on her. At the side of my own vision, Rawlins smiled.

"Some of my clients came here illegally," Carla said. I thought of Lourdes Ortega. Is she a client, Carla? Do you know where she is or what has happened to her? How about her child?

"And I understand that many of you feel, in complete sincerity after careful thought and balancing of complex considerations, that those people deserve no legal niceties. That we should just load them on busses and drop them off at the bullring in Tijuana."

That virtually dared the hard-liners to applaud. Nobody took the bait, but I heard discreet murmurs of agreement at nearby tables.

"Ladies and gentlemen," Carla said, "I'm an American, born in Albuquerque, New Mexico." She emphasized the "New."

"I support the law. I support strong border enforcement. In fact, I currently employ a former Border Patrol agent to help my office with investigation."

Clever, Carla. Sounds great. Means nothing.

I caught O'Laughlin looking my way with malice in his thin smile.

"But let's get real," Carla said. "We have approximately twelve million undocumented immigrants in this country. The biggest

Border Patrol bus I've seen has sixty seats. That's two-hundred thousand busloads of people to run back across the border. And they wouldn't all load up quietly in San Ysidro or Nogales or El Paso. We'd be collecting immigrants in Chicago and New York and Spokane and Tallahassee and Omaha."

Nobody booed. They knew she was right.

"My friends," she said, "it's not going to happen. We're not going to deport twelve million people, even if they broke the law to get here. We're not going to march them onto boxcars at gunpoint. We're not going to cripple a great many American businesses, even if they deserve our scorn for encouraging violations of our law."

The movers and shakers stared at their dessert plates. They knew who ran which businesses. It was not a moment for eye contact. Only Terry O'Laughlin, vigilant bodyguard, glanced from table to table.

Carla went on for fifteen more minutes, mixing statistics with her usual pep talk on the value of immigration and the inevitability of a global labor market. The charm that weakened knees at Tucson High could still work its magic among the skeptical and sometimes cynical proprietors of a wealthy county. My take on the listeners' faces showed at least a grudging approval of her views. In person, she was even better than the Carla Baca seen on TV.

Audience members had written questions on index cards and given them to ushers. Now the chairman read the first question. "You say we cannot send back the twelve million illegal aliens now in the country. Isn't that giving them amnesty for breaking our laws?"

Carla said, "It's not a formal conveyance of amnesty. It simply recognizes reality. As a practical matter, though, it does give them a de facto amnesty, but not a de jure amnesty. There's a big difference. If it's de jure amnesty, that's the law. Those people are here with the blessing of the law. If it's only de facto, then the government retains its option to send back anyone in the group you mentioned for any reason. If the questioner doesn't want those people here, de facto amnesty is the best he can hope for. And in my opinion, that's what will happen."

Finally, the chairman said, "Our last question comes from one of our junior members, Phil Edwards. Well, it's two questions, really. Phil asks, one, if you're married, and two, if you would consider leaving all this controversy behind and running away with him to San Clemente?"

Carla and the crowd laughed. She said, "My answers are, one, no, I'm not married. And two, does Phil know my hourly rate?"

That got her out with more laughs and applause. A dozen people came to the head table and asked for her autograph on their programs. Carla caught the eye of the smitten young deputy and cocked her head toward the door. He approached her and said in a strong voice, "We have to get to the helicopter, Miss Baca."

Carla feigned disappointment. She stood. The crowd parted. The deputy led her out, O'Laughlin walking ahead, looking right and left, Rawlins and me in tow.

Aloft, the three of us headed inland, Rawlins said, "Off to San Clemente with the first guy who can pay, huh? I've been trying to get her down to San Miguel de Allende for months and she won't go."

"Too much happening," Carla said. "But I do want to go sometime."

"I may have to fight that young deputy to take you anywhere," Rawlins said.

She laughed and said in her sweet little girl voice, "Can I fly for a while, Rich?"

"Take it," Rawlins said.

Carla put her left hand on the collective and her right on the cyclic. She eased the collective up and pushed the cyclic forward. She knew what she was doing. We gathered speed and headed north.

"Hey, what about playing by the rules?" I asked. "You don't have a license, do you?"

"I have Rich," she said.

27

At Santa Monica Airport, Rawlins went to a pilot lounge to call his office. Carla and I sat in a conference room that overlooked the runway. The room had phones, a fax machine, a desktop computer, and a projector for travelers who wanted to squeeze in some stimulating PowerPoint between plane rides.

"Did Amric show you the picture of James Delgado?" I said.

"No," Carla said. I looked for telltale recognition of the name, but her expression showed me nothing. I wondered about the always-efficient Amric.

"I can't prove it," I said, "but I feel sure that Lourdes Ortega and her child were with that group in Phoenix. Somehow she got out of the building."

Carla said nothing. Her look said to go on.

"There are lots of possibilities, Carla," I said. "She and the kid might have been taken somewhere else and killed. She might have been killed and the baby taken to be sold, or given to some smuggler's girl who wants a child but can't have one. They might have escaped. They might have been turned loose, although God knows why the bad guys would do that when they killed everyone else."

"What do you want from me?" Carla said.

"Two things. First, I want to see the letter that Lourdes Ortega wrote to you, and whatever you wrote back."

"Why? You saw her letter. There was nothing useful in it, except that she was from Guaymas and she was coming with her husband and child."

"I didn't see it, Carla. I saw another letter from a man in Ensenada. You gave me only Lourdes Ortega's name and told me about the contents of her letter."

"Exactly," she said. "So you know everything I know."

I slammed my hand down on the table. Carla jerked back.

"Listen to me, Carla," I said. "I don't care how you run your law practice. All I care about right now is finding that woman and kid if they're alive."

Carla sat there for a minute, thinking. She stood up and went to a fax machine in the corner. She wrote down the number, then made a cell phone call.

"Amric," she said, "please get the Lourdes Ortega file. There should be an exchange of letters. Two. Fax them to me." She gave him the fax number and hung up. She walked past me, grabbed her purse from the table, and headed for the door.

"So you did answer her," I said.

"I'll be back in a minute," she said.

"My other question, Carla," I said. She stopped and looked at me. "What were you and Rawlins doing in Nogales?"

She turned, opened the door, and left the room.

Carla was gone for ten minutes. The fax chirped and pages rolled into the tray. The first was a cover sheet from Amric, then the letter from Lourdes Ortega. It was just about what Carla had described, but it included a return address. Then I grabbed Carla's answer. It was typed in Spanish.

"Dear Mrs. Oretga," it said, "I received your letter. I advise you not to attempt to enter the United States of America without proper documentation. Please contact my associated firm in Tijuana, Baja California. If you ultimately find yourself in Los Angeles, contact me by telephone or letter when you arrive."

Maybe it would pass legal muster, but it looked to me like a tacit solicitation of people who planned to enter illegally.

Carla came back with Rawlins. They sat together, side by side across the table from me.

"You lied to me, Carla," I said. "You did answer her. You are encouraging people to come here illegally, then you sign them up."

"Just her," Carla said. "I didn't use that last line with the others. It was clear that she was already coming, no matter what."

"Sure," I said. "All that you've accomplished, and you're willing to blow the whole thing by facilitating illegal entries."

"Slow down, Brinker," Rawlins said. "You just made a couple of big assumptions there. You assume that Carla is doing something systematically, rather than as a single act of kindness. Big difference. And you assume that telling someone to contact her later is unlawful, even when that person is sneaking in anyway. You're wrong on both counts. What Carla did was not improper solicitation. The Ortega woman contacted Carla first. Don't be an idiot, sitting across from two experienced attorneys, telling them they don't know the law."

"That's why she kept it secret from her own investigator," I said.

"Carla hadn't seen you or spoken to you since Tucson High School, for heaven's sake," Rawlins said. "Of course she moved cautiously on something so sensitive. But all her cards are on the table now."

Carla Baca just sat there like a quiet client, staring at the table or watching Rawlins.

"Nogales," I said.

"How did you know we were there?" Rawlins asked.

"Luck. I was at a restaurant there," I said, which was true if not complete. "I saw you drive out on the U.S. side. I followed you until you turned off the freeway for the Tucson airport."

"Luck indeed," he said. "Well, we were there. Carla has a network of contacts on both sides of the border. Nothing improper about that. It's perfectly appropriate for someone in her field of practice. We went to see if they knew anything about the Phoenix killings or about Lourdes Ortega."

"Who are the contacts?" I said.

"That doesn't matter," Rawlins said. "Let me remind you that we're supposedly on the same team here. You have ten thousand dollars of Carla's money, plus reimbursement for your expenses. The reason she hired you is because she wants answers."

Carla finally spoke. "It's not the money, Brinker. The point is, my contacts in Nogales have no idea what happened in that house. You can imagine what it's like among immigration people there. No one has talked about much else since it happened. But no one knows any more than we do."

"Why didn't you just call them up?" I said. "You could have saved yourself a trip."

"You know how it works," Rawlins said. "You almost always get better information face to face."

"And you don't get the call intercepted," I said.

Rawlins smiled. "Are you suggesting that we crossed the border for a clandestine sitdown with criminal types? I'm surprised, Brinker. You would never do such a thing, would you?"

"I was on the Border Patrol," I said. "Of course I know some crooks down there. What's your excuse?"

Carla said, "I don't have to make excuses to you if I try to help a person come into this country. Of all people, you should be the most understanding. I know about you and the Avila girl." She looked away when she said it.

When Al Avila and I were on the Border Patrol, we found an abandoned Mexican child living in a sewer pipe connecting the two cities of Nogales. We confirmed that the little girl had not been reported missing. Then we took her to Al and Anna's home in Tucson. Alicia has lived there ever since as the Avilas' child, a sister to their own daughter Anita.

"A six-year-old kid living on her own, surrounded by predators and human waste," I said. "That's a little different than adults sneaking into the country."

Carla said, "Are you still on this case or not?"

"I'm going to find that woman and child, if they're alive," I said. "In spite of you."

Gabi and I went to Ye Olde King's Head on Santa Monica Boulevard, a couple of blocks from the beach. I had a pint of Bass Ale and Gabi sipped a cup of English tea.

"We assume that Lourdes Oretga and the child are alive, right?" Gabi said.

"Right."

"So if we assume that, the question becomes, where is she?"

"She could be anywhere," I said. "Phoenix, here, anywhere in between."

"Exactly. And we'll never know what happened if we can't figure out where that somewhere is."

"Okay."

"So," Gabi said, "I think you need to be looking in places where she's most likely to be. I think that's L.A."

"Because this is where she wanted to come," I said.

"Exactly."

"But that would mean that everything went to hell in Phoenix and she still found a way to get here. Pretty tough."

"I know," Gabi said. "But if someone is holding her prisoner in Phoenix, we have no chance to find her. I'm betting that if somebody saved her, that somebody also helped her go on to her destination."

"Big bet," I said.

Gabi took a sip of my beer. "Maybe I'll have a pint of that," she said.

I flagged the bartender. She drew the Bass from one of about ten taps on the bar. I thought it might be worthwhile to come back here every night and try them all.

"Look," Gabi said. "She told Carla in her letter that she and her family were coming to Los Angeles. And apparently, she was coming with *nada*. There was no talk of having a job, or a relative to help with housing or papers or anything."

"So she needed a place to land," I said. "Someplace to live while she got the child settled and looked for a job."

"And that's where I can help you," Gabi said. "I've done enough stories on immigration and Hispanic issues. I know some places where people go to keep their heads down. I know some people who help them."

"This is such a huge leap," I said. "Eight people get slaughtered and she winds up alive and well in L.A."

"And scared to death," Gabi said. "And surrounded by people who know what scared means. It won't be easy, but it's a way to start."

"It's worth a try," I said.

We sat quietly. I heard darts thunk into boards behind us. The players laughed. A portrait of Winston Churchill observed from the far wall, the old prime minister looking stern in a blue wool suit. The door opened. Cars glided by as if in a silent movie. Gabi scooted closer on her barstool and put her head on my shoulder.

"Instead of this," she said, "you could be back in Tucson, all alone, having a Big Mac for dinner, walking outside to one-hundred-ten degrees."

"Home sweet home," I said.

"My home, too," she said. "What's not to like about this place, though? Well, except for the occasional vicious beating. But you could get that in Tucson, too."

"And I have," I said.

"So come on."

"Talk me into it."

"French dips every day at Phillipe's. Ocean breezes. Full employment for PI's. The Dodgers. Nice pubs like this with unlimited kegs of beer. Passionate sex on demand."

"Your demand or mine?" I asked.

"Yes," she said.

28

If you're Hispanic and want to get lost, East Los Angeles would be hard to beat. Somebody told me that East L.A. is the biggest Hispanic community in the United States. I believe that. Its borders are elastic. It covers several cities, not just the section of Los Angeles that lies east of downtown. People move in and out. Many move up. But much of the population is stable, generations of Mexican-Americans dating their families' time in East L.A. to the late 1800's.

"I should go with you," Gabi said. "I've built up trust with Fidelia. It could save you lots of time and small talk."

"I still give off Border Patrol vibes," I said. "I'll take any help I can get to win friends there."

We took my car and headed inland on the I-10. Gabi gave me directions to skirt the edge of downtown, cut north to Sixth, then follow it east across the river. It became Whittier Boulevard, the Main Street of East L.A. Cars jammed the roadway, some cruising, most seeming purposefully bound for work or home. Pedestrians moved busily along the sidewalks from *farmacia* to *panadería* to *carnicería*.

"There's a shorter way in," Gabi said, "but this gives you a sense of the place. The size, the number of people, all the history along the boulevard."

"How does a little widow lady come by all her knowledge and influence here?" I asked.

"Many years and a little money," Gabi said. "She was an elementary school teacher for forty years. Her husband was a mailman. Those were terrific jobs for Mexican-Americans in those days. Security, okay pay, retirement benefits. And respect. They saved their money and made some modest investments."

"Around their own neighborhood," I said.

"Exactly. Nothing huge, but they helped people buy houses, or start little shops, or get through a rough patch. When the neighborhoods went to hell after the riots in the late sixties, a few extra dollars for people was heaven sent."

"You get all this from clips at the paper?"

"No," she said. "Fidelia has never been interviewed. Heaven knows I've tried. She tells everyone that she wants no publicity. But if you walk down Whittier Boulevard and ask ten people who the best person in all of Los Angeles is, six or seven will name her."

"Maybe she's the real *nuestra señora del norte*," I said.

"Maybe so."

"How old is this saint?"

"She admits to eighty," Gabi said. "She's been admitting to that for a long time."

We turned north off the boulevard and crept along a narrow street of modest stucco houses. The walks were swept clean. Flowers bloomed in little gardens and hanging baskets on porches. Most places had small lawns in front. Children played in groups of two or three. An adult watched every group.

"It's not all like this," Gabi said. "There are huge pockets of poverty and neglect. But if you live on Fidelia's street, you better mow your grass and sweep your driveway. Your windows better gleam."

Fidelia Ramos's house was white stucco, painted recently, with fresh Santa Fe green trim on the window casings and the door. The front window sparkled in the morning sunlight. A young man sat in a rocking chair on the porch. He had a Doberman sitting on each side of him. He stood as we approached. The Dobermans didn't move. The man was medium height with black hair cut short.

Muscles rippled in a tight T-shirt. The shirt bore a sixties-looking picture of a man and the words, "Ruben Salazar 1928-1970."

"Gabi," he said, all smiles.

"Diego," Gabi said. They hugged. "This is Brinker. Brink, this is Diego, Fidelia's son."

We shook hands. Diego said, "Mr. Brinker, would you mind?" He held his arms away from his body. I took the hint, assumed the position, and he patted me down quickly. I had followed Gabi's advice and left my gun in the car.

"Thank you," he said. He looked to Gabi.

"Don't tell me," she said.

Diego laughed. "No, no. Mamá said absolutely not. *No es decente.* Please come in."

Fidelia Ramos sat in a large wingback chair that faced her front window. Her hair was gray, pulled back in what my mother used to call a bun. Her dress was black. She was a tiny thing who could have fit the two Dobermans on the chair with her. She did not rise when Diego led us in, but her wrinkled face lost twenty years when she smiled her welcome. She held out her arms and Gabi knelt for a hug.

"*Abuela*," Gabi said. Grandmother. Gabi had told me that Fidelia wanted her friends, not only her grandchildren, to call her by that term of endearment and respect.

"Gabriela, *que linda eres.*" How pretty you are. Fidelia's voice was strong and filled with the happiness that old ladies feel when meeting young ladies worthy of their approval.

They chattered away in Spanish for a few moments, too quickly and quietly for me to follow. I looked around the room. It was filled with family photographs, dozens of them. They spanned generations. Some must have been Fidelia's great-grandchildren. One showed Diego in Marine Corps dress uniform. He wore an impressive cluster of ribbons and rifle and pistol expert medals. He looked so young yet so formidable. Finally, Gabi turned to me, took my hand, and drew me forward.

"And you are Mr. Brinker," Fidelia said. She spoke English with no accent that I could discern. "I should be angry at you."

"Why is that, Señora Ramos?" I said. I hoped I hadn't committed some blunder already.

"Because I thought, maybe someday, I would match up my youngest son, Diego there, and Gabriela."

"Mamá," Diego said. He looked at me and shrugged, as if to say, what can I do?

Fidelia said, "But old souls don't plan such things these days. Young hearts do. Please call me *abuela*, Mr. Brinker. If Gabriela loves you, I will think of you as family."

Gabi blushed. I said, "Thank you, *abuela*."

Diego pushed two chairs to the side of the window so Fidelia could talk with us and still keep an eye on her street. We sat.

"Diego," Fidelia said, "please bring the pitcher of iced coffee from the refrigerator. Only ten o'clock in the morning and so hot."

Diego went into the kitchen and returned quickly with the coffee and three ice-filled glasses. He poured for all of us, left the pitcher by his mother, and walked outside to the front porch. We sipped our coffee. I flashed back to drinking iced tea in Riverside on another hot morning. Where was Sandra Liebowitz Brown?

Fidelia said, "The story Gabriela told me, that's a terrible thing."

"It happens too often," I said. "Not so much in houses, but on the travel routes out in the desert."

"Yes, the desert," she said. "You know, many years ago, we had a man on the television here. No Telemundo or Univision then. His name was Jerry Dunphy. So very handsome, I thought. Always a twinkle in his eye. He died a few years ago. When he started his news program every night, he always said, 'From the desert to the sea, to all of Southern California, a good evening.' I think maybe he understood that it's all the same, from the desert to the sea. Dangers everywhere, but opportunities, too. And we're all together in life, no matter whether we're struggling across the desert or playing by the sea."

"I think so," Gabi said.

Fidelia turned back to me.

She said, "You were *la migra*."

"Yes, I was," I said.   That's probably the end of this conversation, I thought.

The old woman picked up on my reaction.

"It's all right," she said. "I'm not opposed to borders. We need laws. I don't encourage breaking them. Do you understand that, Mr. Brinker?"

"Yes," I said.

"And you, Gabriela?"

"Of course, *abuela*," Gabi said.

"It's important to me that everyone knows this," Fidelia said. "That way, when I help people in need, everyone will understand that my heart is good. Even if the people who need help are not always complying with the laws. All people are entitled to kindness. Mary and Joseph were weary travelers, and Mary was with child."

She watched me closely as she spoke. I nodded and she smiled. Then she turned to Gabi.

"Gabriela," she said, "this is not for the newspaper. Do we agree?"

"Yes, of course," Gabi said.

"If something happens later that you can't avoid reporting, then I know that you have certain obligations. But the history of whatever you learn stops before it reaches back to me."

"I understand," Gabi said.

Fidelia took another sip of coffee. "I had some fine coffee from Chiapas, close to Guatemala, but we drank it all," she said. "This is just something from Target on the boulevard. I hope you like it."

"It's perfect," I said.

"The next time you visit, perhaps my friends will have brought me more from Chiapas or maybe Oaxaca."

"Make them hurry," Gabi said, "because we'd like to come back soon."

Fidelia beamed, then her expression turned serious. She shifted a bit in her seat and pursed her lips.

"Now," she said, "to this business of the woman and her child."

I held my breath. Gabi folded her hands in her lap. We waited.

141

"Actually, you know," Fidelia said, "I should have said 'her children.' She has a little one with her, and like Mary, she's pregnant."

"Do you know if this is Lourdes Ortega from Guaymas?" I asked.

"People think I know everything," she said. "Sometimes, though, I find it's best to know only what's necessary. What I told you is enough for me to have helped the woman, and enough for you to take the next step in your work."

"Thank you," I said.

"Diego will give you a telephone number," Fidelia said. "Call tomorrow, not today. The person who answers will be expecting you. I have arranged this for you. He will do what I ask. There is something you must do for me to show your trust."

I wondered how to answer, but Gabi said at once, "Brinker will do whatever you ask, *abuela*."

"*¿Verdad?*" Fidelia said. Truly?

"*De acuerdo*," I said. Of course.

She gave us her grandmotherly smile of approval. "When you go where I have arranged, you must not bring a weapon. Not even in your car. Gabriela has told me that you were attacked. I realize that my request is a very serious matter. You are no longer a stranger to me, but you will be to the people who help me. This is how you show trust. When you go, you will have my protection. Everyone understands that you are not to be harmed, and consequences will result if you are. But you will be searched. That's only reasonable. If you have a weapon, it will be taken from you and you'll be turned away. You will be safe, but your search for this woman will be over. After that, I can do nothing more for you."

"I'll do as you say," I said.

We were silent for a moment. Fidelia looked out her window and said to no one in particular, "It's so much more difficult now than when I was young. We could do what was necessary to help people. Now, with the drugs and the terrible killing gangs, so much money and so much hatred. I just don't know."

She turned back to face us. She smiled at Gabi and said, "He's a very nice boy, Gabriela. May God bless the two of you."

The front door opened. Diego held it for us as we left. The Dobermans held their positions, on guard. Diego handed me a yellow sticky note with a phone number written in pencil.

"Learn it and burn it," he said.

Gabi and I drove south on Euclid, crossing Whittier Boulevard, headed for the freeway.

"Wow," I said. "It's like Molly Goldberg meets Don Corleone."

"The Godmother," Gabi said. "Somebody called her that once. She laughed for the rest of the afternoon."

"I think she's the real *nuestra señora*," I said.

"Don't tell Carla," Gabi said.

"I'll have her protection," I said. "What does that mean? Someone gets rough with me, then Fidelia has them kneecapped?"

Gabi said, "In her case, I think it means nobody will get rough with you. It's a funny thing in that macho society. A little old woman like that does a lot of good for decades, and her word becomes law. It's like everyone is a kid in her house. You sin if you don't obey her. I think even drug dealers would do what she says, at least the locals. They know that disrespecting her would turn the whole community against them."

"Including some guys who could hurt them."

"Exactly."

"Hard to picture little *abuela* Fidelia ordering a hit," I said.

"It is," Gabi said. "But when you've been around here a while, it's easy to imagine anyone following the order. Anyway, the word on the boulevard is that Diego handles things when they get rough."

"He looks like he could do it," I said. "You notice the marksmanship medals?"

"A doting son and a straight shooter," Gabi said. "Fidelia probably doesn't even have to ask. He just knows what she needs."

We were up on the I-10 now. East L.A.'s smoggy heat rippled in my rear view mirror. Ahead of us, the soaring downtown skyline.

143

"You know," Gabi said, "the Molly Goldberg thing is almost true. They used to have a big Jewish community in East L.A. There were lots of little enclaves of European immigrants there. When they did well, they moved. Lots of them went to West L.A. They formed new communities around Fairfax and what's Century City now and Santa Monica."

"Opportunity," I said.

"You know that famous deli on Fairfax. Canter's. Everybody thinks it's been there forever. But it started in Boyle Heights when so many Jews lived there."

"You're an East L.A. historian," I said.

"Yeah, well, now I'm a Latina at the marina," she said. "It's great. But I can't get over how comfortable I am in a little old stucco house in the Mexican neighborhood."

"You're exactly where the European immigrants were a couple of generations ago," I said.

Gabi said, "Whenever I try to lure you over here, I'm always talking about the west side. The beach and the restaurants and all the sweet life stuff. I never say 'come see my roots in the barrio' and we'll have *menudo*."

"I'd do anything for you," I said, "except eat *menudo*. *Posole*, that would be okay."

"I'm serious, Brink."

"I know," I said. "I know where you're from. I grew up in the same town. Your parents knew my parents. You're not sneaking anything past me."

"My parents are all alone back home," Gabi said. She laughed. "The only Mexican family in history to have just one kid, and she leaves them."

"They want you to be here, no matter how much they miss you," I said. "They left Mexico so you could reach as high as you want."

She leaned back against the headrest. She closed her eyes. In a few moments, she sighed.

"It's ridiculous for me think my life is complicated," she said.

"Why?"

"If my parents hadn't come north before I was born, I could have been one of the people in that house in Phoenix."

I took my right hand off the wheel and reached over to her. She grasped my hand in both of hers. We stayed that way, not speaking as the freeway led us around the downtown core and then west toward Santa Monica.

"What do you think Diego meant when he said times are crazy?" I said.

"I think one of the family projects got messy," Gabi said. "If you're helping illegal immigrants, it's bound to happen occasionally. And it fits with the Phoenix disaster. If Fidelia knows where those people are now, she knows that something bad happened there."

"What happens when I call this phone number?" I asked.

"You'll get run through a couple of cutouts, so they can cover their tracks," Gabi said. "Then, I think, you'll meet the elusive and lucky Lourdes Ortega."

29

The man who answered the phone spoke only Spanish. He gave me another number to call. An English speaker picked up, took my cell number, and said, "You will be contacted."

We were in Gabi's apartment, sitting at the table in her small kitchen. I said, "Two cutouts so far. You know your way around this business."

"Fidelia did this once before with me," she said. "Some poor woman came to an emergency room, bleeding from the head, having seizures. The staff just left her there for hours. She died. We couldn't get anyone to talk about it. Fidelia knew a woman who worked there and saw what happened. I had to go through two phone numbers and a secret rendezvous to get the interview."

I sat around all day, waiting for a call. Nothing. It came at six-thirty the next morning. Gabi was gone already, bound for a story in the far reaches of the San Fernando Valley. I was clearing the little breakfast table and loading the dishwasher.

"Leave now," the voice said. Male. No accent that I could identify. "Alone. Go to Redlands. You know where that is?"

"Yes," I said.

"Follow the signs to the university. There's a big green lawn with a church at the end. Drive down there and park in front of a building called Fairmont. Lock your car and walk over to the big lawn. Sit down on the grass and wait there. Call nobody. You'll be contacted. Got it?"

"Yes," I said. The caller hung up.

I thought about my gun but decided to follow Fidelia's order. Stupid of me, but I felt compelled by the moral authority of the old woman. I put the gun in a bedroom bureau drawer, under Gabi's sweaters.

L.A. rush hour was well underway. When wasn't it? I figured at least an hour to downtown and another hour-plus to Redlands, out I-10 past San Bernardino. The newsreader on KFWB said the La Habra Heights fire was contained, but firefighters worried about gusty winds in the forecast. A dozen homes had been destroyed. From five miles north, I couldn't see the plumes of smoke that had been present for days. You could tell, though. The air all around me was gray and sour.

Two-and-a-half hours after leaving the marina, I took the Orange Street exit and drove a few blocks north to Colton Avenue. Redlands looked like a city in transition, with rundown postwar homes and check cashing services on one block, but new business going up nearby. The university could have been an Ivy transplanted to a land of groves and growth. The old stone administration building sat atop a hill at one end of a sweeping green quad. From there, you could look down to the chapel, with the mountains barely visible a few miles away in the smoggy background.

I drove toward the chapel, circled around, and saw the Fairmont sign. It was a dormitory. Most of the buildings lining the quad appeared to be dorms. This was summer, so not many people were about. I parked in the shade of an enormous California oak, one of many around the quad. I walked onto the lawn, and sat to wait.

They're pretty smart, I thought. I was alone, utterly exposed, in a vast green open space. Fidelia's crew could check me out from a dozen vantage points. They could spot me from the hilltop administration building, or from shadowed spots between the dorms that neighbored Fairmont. They could cruise along Colton and have a look. I hoped that no snipers were invited to this meeting.

Four kids in a banged up Honda Accord cruised slowly around the quad. Two males, two females, all Anglo. They looked at me without interest as they drove by.

A man driving a university pickup truck with a riding mower in back eased past my car and pulled in at one of the dorms near Colton Avenue. He parked in the shade and sipped a soda from a bright red can. I wondered if he was really a groundsman or a watcher. Paranoia runs deep.

I heard laughter behind me. Three young people carrying musical instrument cases emerged from a building next to the chapel. Two trumpets and a trombone, I thought. Somebody had told me that Redlands had a famous music program. The musicians climbed into a Highlander hybrid SUV and drove past without noticing me.

Ten minutes passed before I saw another soul. Across the quad, a young couple strolled along the sidewalk and up the stairs to another dorm. The girl was patting the guy's butt. I didn't remember anyone doing that to me when I was in college. Born too soon.

Another half hour passed. A van turned off Colton and drove slowly along the quad. It was the kind with no windows on the side except for those by the front seat. "Sanchez Landscaping, San Bernardino" and a phone number were professionally painted on the sliding side door. The driver kept his eyes on me, not the road.

The van turned left at the chapel, then again at the edge of the quad. It stopped near me. The side door slid open. A young Hispanic man said, "Get in." I climbed in. The man slid the door shut and we began to move. A partition shielded the driver and the front view. With no natural light, the rear compartment was nearly dark. A small overhead bulb provided a faint glow.

"*¿Tiene armas?*" the man said.

"No," I said. And in Spanish, "Fidelia told me not to bring a gun. I honor her wish."

He gave me a cursory pat down anyway. We rode for ten minutes. It was slow, stop and go. I heard almost no other traffic. We had to be on neighborhood streets, I thought. Definitely not the freeway or even a busy local road.

Finally, the van slowed and turned, taking a little dip like you find at the end of driveways. We crept forward and the engine sound echoed slightly, then shut down. A garage? I heard the noise of a small electric motor and a door rolling down. When it thunked closed, my guard pushed open the van door and beckoned me out.

It was two-car garage. A light blue Corolla took the other space. My guard knocked on the door leading into the house. After a few moments, we heard footsteps coming toward us.

The door opened and Sandra Liebowitz Brown said, "It is you."

I was too surprised to answer her.

She said, "I wondered when they told me the name, but I couldn't make the connection between my brother and Lourdes. I still can't."

"Neither can I," I said. "We have things to talk about."

"Yes," she said. "But first, you'll want to meet Lourdes."

She led me through a laundry room and kitchen. The washer and dryer and dishwasher all were running. I heard a gasoline-powered lawn mower humming away in the back yard. In the living room, a pregnant woman sat on a sofa with a little girl. The girl held a tiny gray dog that might have been a poodle or a Lhasa Apso or a bit of both. A cup and a big box of Kleenex were on the coffee table.

Sandra Liebowitz Brown said, "Irma, *¿quieres venir conmigo?* Scooby *también.*" The child looked at her mother. Lourdes smiled and nodded her approval. The girl put the dog on the sofa cushion and followed Sandra. Scooby jumped down and chased both of them into the hall.

Lourdes Ortega was short and slender. I might have said "frail" but her abdomen gave her some bulk. She managed a small nervous smile as I took a chair opposite her. She must have been told that Fidelia sent me, but perhaps I still gave off that scent of Border Patrol that illegal immigrants often noticed. Or maybe what she had seen in Phoenix would leave her frightened for years to come.

I said in Spanish, "I am so glad to find you and Irma safe."

"*Gracias a Dios,*" she said.

"I understand this will be painful," I said, "and I'm sorry. But I need to know what happened."

149

She looked down at her folded hands. She might have been recalling the story of her journey, or deciding how much to tell me.

"The trip went well," she said. "We took a bus from Guaymas to Nogales. Then we found the guides near the fence. We paid them. It was all our money for the three of us."

She patted her tummy. "Four," she said, smiling.

I said, "Everything was fine on the way to Phoenix?"

"Yes," she said. "At dark, we were driven outside of Nogales to where the big iron fence ends. The guides took us through the barbed wire. They cut some for me because it's too difficult for me to get low on the ground and go under."

She sipped coffee. Can you drink coffee when you're pregnant? I had no idea. We heard Irma laughing down the hall. Lourdes smiled again. She seemed remarkably at ease for what she had been through.

"A van was waiting near the fence. The ride to Phoenix was very fast," she said. "We kept looking for the immigration or some other police, but nobody bothered us. We came to Phoenix late at night, I think."

One of my guards strolled through the living room. He carried two beer cans. Pabst Blue Ribbon. I didn't know they still made it. He pushed open the sliding glass door and walked into the back yard. The lawn mower had stopped running.

"The house was like a prison camp," Lourdes said. "They put us all in one bedroom. I could not understand that because there were other bedrooms. We could see them when we went to the toilet down the hall. There was one little bed. Everyone said I should take it because I am pregnant. Irma slept there with me. Pablo slept on the floor beside us, if he slept at all."

"I'm very sorry for what happened to him," I said.

"Thank you," she said. "But it's okay."

"What?" I said. How could she say such a thing only a couple weeks after what happened in Phoenix?

"We all went together with the new guides," he said. "The men left as soon as we crossed the Colorado River. They had farm work there, they said. The driver said it was California then. He laughed because there is a place where cars usually must stop for inspection. But he knew it would be closed when we came."

"Just the two men got out there?" I said.

"Yes. The young woman, Dulce was her name, was still in the van when we were brought here."

Lourdes spoke up. "Dulce was very sad. Something bad happened to her at the house, before we left. But she wouldn't speak of it."

"Can you tell me what you mean?" I said.

"The boss took her away," Pablo said. "We did not see her again until we were all in the van to leave. She was crying and looked so sad. But she would say nothing."

"Maybe if I, a woman, had been the only person there," Lourdes said. "But with men, it was too awful to speak of, I think."

"But all of you who started the trip in Mexico made it away from Phoenix?" I said.

"Yes," they answered in unison.

"You don't know where Dulce was going?"

"No," Lourdes said. "She never told anyone."

I took two photographs from my pocket. The first was the driver license shot of James Delgado. I held it over the table so both Lourdes and Pablo could see it.

"Do you recognize this man?"

Both shook their heads and said, "No."

The other picture was the one Al had given me, the photo being circulated quietly by Phoenix police. I placed it on the table.

Lourdes gasped. Pablo said, "*Sí. El jefe.*"

I said, "This is the man who showed up in Phoenix and took command?"

"He is the one who led Dulce away," Lourdes said.

"Later, he put us all in the van and sent us to California," Pablo said.

"He didn't come with you, though?"

"No," Pablo said. "Two new men brought us from Phoenix. They took turns driving."

"You were going to Los Angeles. Did anyone say why they brought you here?"

Lourdes and Pablo looked at each other, as if to ask if one had heard something the other missed. They both said no.

"Had either of you been in touch with Fidelia or Sandra before you came here?"

Pablo said, "No."

"But Lourdes, you had written to Carla Baca, hadn't you?"

"Yes. She wrote back to me and said to contact her when we arrived. But we have not been allowed to call or write to anyone."

"I understand," I said. I stood to leave.

"Sir," Pablo said. "We were told that we could trust you not to report us to the immigration. Is that true?"

"I promised Fidelia," I said. "You've given me information that may help the police solve the crimes in Phoenix, and I should tell them the facts. But I will not tell them who you are or where you are."

Sandra Liebowitz Brown, behind me, said, "Tomorrow, they'll be someplace else. But we need to keep this house a secret."

"Don't worry about me," I said. "I don't even know where this house is."

"Good," she said.

Pablo and Lourdes took Irma and the dog to play in the back yard. Sandra Brown made coffee. We sat at the kitchen table.

"So this is where you've been for a few days," I said.

"Yes," she said. "I'm sorry for ignoring your calls. It was made clear to me that this situation was urgent."

"Who made it clear?" I said.

"I told you that I volunteer with local aid groups," she said. "This one's unofficial, I guess you could say. People who help others occasionally need someone in a particular area to step up. My house isn't far from here, so I got the job."

"You do this a lot, with illegal immigrants and a safe house?"

"Enough," she said.

David Katz's lawyer brain can absorb seemingly contradictory or unconnected facts, information flying at him from several directions, and rapidly sort it all into a coherent whole. I can't do that without taking a long time to think. But I can listen to a witness and make a good guess about the person's honesty. I had no doubt that Sandra Brown had been telling me the truth. If the truth would hurt, she simply wouldn't speak.

"Did your brother know about this?" I said.

"Joseph knew that I do volunteer work, of course," she said. I remembered that she always called her brother Joseph instead of José. "But not this work in particular, no."

"It's Fidelia who sets up these assignments for you, isn't it?"

She shrugged.

"Did your brother know Fidelia?"

"I don't believe so," she said.

"You can't think of any possible connection between what happened to him and this work you do with illegal immigrants?"

"It never even occurred to me," she said. "Not until they told me someone named Brinker was coming here. Then I wondered about a connection. But I can't imagine what it would be. Carla is about the only thing that Lourdes and Pablo have in common with Joseph."

"Only Carla," I said.

"But it's ridiculous to think she had anything to do with the deaths," Sandra said. "All she did was help people. I admire her very much. Joseph adored her."

"So did I," I said.

31

The guards loaded me back in the van and returned me to the Redlands campus. The temperature was pushing a hundred. The groundsman who had arrived earlier was riding his mower over the long lawn that fronted the dorms. I opened my car windows, started the engine, and let the air conditioner blow. The trees offered plenty of shade. I sat on the lawn and thought about what I knew and what I didn't know.

Lourdes Ortega and her family were safe. Maybe Carla Baca encouraged them to sneak into the country, but at least it didn't get them killed. I struggled to connect the Phoenix murders with the deaths of José Liebowitz and Bo Bergstrom. Who were the Phoenix victims? Police Chief Kalven knew, but I didn't.

Maybe there was no connection. But Carla's relationships with the two victims and the illegal immigrants made for a powerful coincidence. And now Liebowitz's sister had turned up as an underground helper for Fidelia.

Smog percolated in the heat as I pointed the car toward Los Angeles. The mountains north of town had vanished in the heavy gray air. It's like my view of the case, I thought.

Eduardo Salvador was involved with the house in Phoenix. Okay, but how? Was he just another smuggler? Was he Dulce's rapist, if there was a rape? Or was he the savior suggested by his name? A good guy who got the illegal immigrants safely out of that house before murderers or *la migra* appeared?

My fuel gauge said I was almost running on empty. I pulled off the freeway at Covina, gassed up, and bought a bottle of orange juice. I called Vicente, Hector Ortiz's man in Nogales. He answered on the second ring. I heard canned music and indistinct public address announcements behind him.

"This phone okay to ask you some questions?" I said.

"Never a good idea," Vicente said.

"I don't have time to come down to Nogales," I said.

"You're in luck," he said. "I just got off a plane at LAX. You want to have a beer?"

"Sure."

"Okay," he said. "It'll take me a while to get my bag and get a car. You know that place we met before, not far from here?"

It had been more than three years, but I remembered the spot.

"Yes," I said.

"One hour," he said. The call went dead.

It took longer than I expected, like everything in L.A. traffic. The bar was near Century and Crenshaw, east of the Hollywood Park race track. A sign in the window said, "Sorry, we're open."

Vicente sat at a small table in the back. None of the afternoon drinkers bothered him. People seldom bothered Vicente. He was sipping a Bud from the bottle and watching the door when I walked in.

"Your being in town a coincidence?" I said.

"Yeah," he said. "Combination business and pleasure trip. Nothing to do with the stuff you asked us about."

Vicente was a U.S. citizen with no criminal convictions, although every fed west of the Mississippi had to know that he worked for Hector Ortiz. With his citizenship and clean record, he moved freely across the border.

"You know a guy named Eduardo Salvador?" I asked.

"Not personally," he said. "I know who he is, what he does."

A waitress who looked about Fidelia Ramos's age came over and stood by the table. Vicente held up his bottle and two fingers. She went away without a word.

"Since I saw you and Hector, some things have happened. I spent days trying to find out if a family connected to my client got killed in Phoenix. It turns out that they're safe. Eduardo Salvador apparently got them and some other people from Phoenix to California."

"And you're inviting me to the humanitarian award ceremony," Vicente said.

"I need to find out what happened in that house," I said.

The waitress came back with two Buds for us and a glass for me.

"Why?" Vicente said. "Sounds to me like everything's cool. The family's alive. Your client doesn't have to worry about them now. Forget it. Make a donation to the Border Patrol Benevolent Fund in Salvador's name and let it go."

"Lot of reasons not to," I said. "That house was filled with bodies. Four more were found out on the reservation. The Phoenix police chief knows I've been on the case. He figures I owe him. If my client played fast and loose with me on this, maybe I can't trust her on other things."

"Hmmm," Vicente said.

"And I had two hoods try to beat me up, and some Nogales freelancer I don't even know shows up to blow them away. I need to be better informed here."

"I know about Jimmy Delgado. He shoots straight, I hear."

"You know that guy?"

"Sure."

"You wouldn't happen to know where he is? I'd like to talk to him. I might learn something about this case."

Vicente smiled, tilted back his bottle, and downed most of the beer.

"I know exactly where he is," he said.

I waited. Sometimes it's good to let him enjoy the moment before pushing harder.

Finally, I said, "Where?"

"He's in a place we keep in Nogales. Mexican side. Frida and Maria take turns going over there, making him feel welcome. They think a twenty-four-year old hitman with U.S. citizenship and access to Hector's liquor stash is pretty erotic."

"How come Hector's sitting on Delgado?" I said.

"Because we put him on you," Vicente said.

Now it was my turn for a long pull on the beer.

"Why?" I said.

"Hector says he owes you for life."

"I've told him he doesn't," I said. "He paid that off long ago."

"He'll keep paying anyway. Hector doesn't choose sides for a day. Relationships with him are permanent."

"For better or worse," I said.

"Right," Vicente said. "When you left that Sunday, he said to me, 'That dumb son of a bitch is gonna get himself killed. Let's find some friend to keep an eye on him in the states.' So I remembered Jimmy D. He'd done small jobs for us, but he really wants to be a high quality Mexican hoodlum, you know?"

"He was on me the next day in Los Angeles."

"Right. He called us from Tucson airport. Said you were checked in for LAX. I told him to get on the plane with you. Get on the same rental car bus and try to tail you. If he lost you, he could pick you up later at Marina del Rey."

"Let's have an understanding about that right now," I said. "I want to keep Gabi clear."

"Relax," Vicente said. "I just wanted him to know where you were. That was good to do, because he lost you in traffic coming out of the airport. He picked you up at the marina that afternoon. That's how he spotted those guys tailing you. He said they were pretty pissed off when you got a helicopter on top of a parking garage."

"Just leave Gabi out of it," I said.

"We're protecting you, so obviously we're not gonna hurt her. Why would we? You've got my personal word on that."

"Okay," I said.

"I can't speak for the bad guys, though," he said. "You might wanna use caution and have Señorita Corona do the same."

"So what happened after the shooting?"

"Jimmy calls. He's completely fucked up, almost crying. He wants to be a real crook, but acing a couple of barrio gangbangers turned out to be freakier than he expected. Some people just aren't cut out for this work. I told him to get his ass into Mexico fast. He drove down to Tijuana, ditched the rental, bought a jalopy, and took the scenic Mexican roads to Nogales."

"What are you going to do with him?"

"Well, Hector wasn't exactly looking for another dependent, you know? But the kid did just what we told him. I said, 'You see that Brinker doesn't get hurt.' He did that. So we'll give him a job where he can't do much damage. Maybe he'll gain wisdom with experience."

"He can't go back to the states," I said. "The L.A. county sheriff put a want on him. He's probably on the FBI list by now."

"Right. He'll do okay with us. He's got Spanish, he's not a doper, he takes orders really seriously. His mom can just walk across the border and back, nice and legal, when she wants to visit him. And I guarantee you, after a few days with Frida and María, he'll have no pent-up sexual frustration to cloud his judgment."

"So what about the other guys tailing me? Any idea where they came from?"

A couple of sixtyish men wearing old Lakers jackets strolled in and looked around. The Lakers used to play at the Forum, just a few blocks from here. I wondered if these were neighborhood guys who felt robbed when the team moved to Staples Center. They sat near the front and paid no attention to us. Vicente had watched them, but now he looked reassured and turned back to me.

"Part of this I know," he said. "Part of it I'm guessing. A lot of the immigration runs to California have two legs. North to Tucson or Phoenix, then west to San Diego or L.A. or wherever. Eduardo Salvador is a west leg guy. His people don't bring anyone through the fence. They pick up the job in Arizona, scout the roadblocks on I-8 or I-10, then take the travelers on the last leg."

"Okay," I said.

"The thing is, they get those jobs two ways. One way, they come into the halfway house and take over. Sometimes they just pass the word and the original crew runs like hell. They steal from the *coyotes* and demand more money from the *pollos*. People with no money get left on their own, halfway to their destination."

"Nice guys," I said. *Pollos* is what smugglers call the people they're guiding into the states. It means "chickens."

"Anybody doesn't like their deal and puts up a fight," Vicente said, "they just shoot 'em. Sometimes they get a choice. *Plata o plumbo.*"

"Silver or lead," I said.

"Right. They can take the money or take a bullet. Lot of money or lots of bullets. It's usually a pretty easy call."

"Maybe that's what happened in Phoenix. But you and Hector warned me off the idea of a gang rivalry."

"Right. Because a new crew usually takes over with a deal. It's set up way in advance. That way the guys who know the fence do all their work there, getting people across. The guys who know the U.S. highways stick to that. Kind of like doctors. You know, specialists."

"That's what Eduardo Salvador does?"

Vicente smiled, drained the last of his beer, and stood up. He leaned down to me and said very quietly, "That's what he's supposed to do. Think about what Hector and I told you that Sunday. I'm not repeating it here. And get the tab for the beers, will you?"

I said, "Do you still have somebody on me?"

"Don't waste a lot of time and energy looking for him," he said.

"So you think I'm still being tailed."

"Jimmy took out two," he said. "You ever see that old sci-fi movie on TV? 'Them.' That's the name of it. 'Them.' The idea was, you kill one monster, and two more take its place right away."

He headed for the door. Two hard-looking guys were coming in. They stepped aside as Vicente passed.

32

Gabi stood barefoot at her balcony railing, looking out over the marina. Boaters were returning to port just in time for happy hour. A cluster of them moved slowly around the breakwater guarding the marina entrance. Even on the water, L.A. has traffic jams. She turned around as I walked to the balcony.

I said, "I'd crawl across the desert in August for that smile."

She stood on tiptoes and I still had to bend down to kiss her. I put my arms around her waist, picked her up, and squeezed hard as she pressed her face against my neck.

"Wow," she said. "Sweet talk and chiropractic, too."

"I hardly saw you this morning," I said. "It seems like a whole day without you. Not a good thing."

"Nice to know," she said. "I had the same thought."

I put her down. She led me inside to the living room sofa. Gabi looked edgy.

"What's the matter?" I said.

"I think somebody tried to break in here today," she said.

I wonder how many thoughts the human brain can process in an instant. I had seen no damage on the door when I let myself in. Gabi was not hurt. I recalled the beating she took when she helped me on another case. I would do anything to keep her safe. Maybe this line of work was no longer for me, now that someone else was part of me.

"What happened?" I said.

"My neighbor two doors down, Christi, came home early today. She usually works until five or six at Sony in Culver City. Today she had a cold or flu or something, so she left at noon. When the elevator door opened, she saw a guy bent over my doorknob, fiddling with keys. He jerked right up when he heard the elevator. Christi asked if she could help him. He said, 'Oh, I must have the wrong apartment.' Then he walked fast away from her to the stairwell."

"She call the cops?"

"No. She called the manager, but he said there was nothing he could do. She didn't have my cell number, so she left a message on my machine here."

"What did this guy look like?"

"Christi said young. Hispanic, she thought. Short hair. Pretty well dressed, all in black or really dark blue. She was feeling lousy so she wasn't sharp, but she got that much."

"That sure sounds like one of the men who tailed me from Carla's office that morning," I said. "If so, two of his pals are dead. I hope I see him before he sees me."

We sat in silence, thinking it over. There was no sense in asking Gabi to go hide in Tucson or get an out-of-town assignment for a couple of weeks. She wasn't foolhardy, but she was offended by intimidation.

After a few minutes, I told her about the trip to Redlands, the Ortega family's story, Dulce, and Vicente.

"I'll sleep a lot better knowing that all those people got out of the house alive," I said. "But I don't feel an inch closer to putting this case together."

"You are, though," Gabi said. "You know where James Delgado came from. And you know he won't be back."

"Someone took his place, though. And I still have to worry about the other guys. This attempted break-in sounds like they're still around and cranking it up a notch. Vicente was no help in identifying whoever wants me roughed up."

"Why is he here?" Gabi said.

"I don't know. He said it had nothing to with what I'm working on."

"You believe him?"

"Vicente is Hector's go-to guy for lots of things," I said. "Or he could just have a girl friend over here. A little time off for Frida and María. Who knows?"

Gabi nodded but said nothing. I could see her drifting off to that quiet place where she thinks about tricky problems. She'd be back soon with an answer. Meanwhile, I reached over and held her hand. The door to the balcony was open. I heard the putt-putt of boats coming under power to their berths, and laughter as the crews tied up and headed for the bars.

"We still agree that Carla is the key, right?" Gabi said.

"She'll have to do," I said. "I've got nothing else."

"Okay. If you wanted to find out as much as you could about me, who would you ask? Not my parents or my editor or Christi down the hall. Who would you ask?"

"Me," I said.

"Exactly," she said. "So if you want to probe Carla, pardon the expression, who you gonna call?"

"You mean Rawlins?"

"Right."

"No good, Gabi," I said. "That guy is nuts about her. He'd tell me anything to make her look good or keep her out of trouble."

"You're a skilled interrogator, babe."

"So is he."

"Look," she said. "We wondered if she might be involved with people smuggling. Maybe she is, and Rawlins knows it. He wants to keep her from harm. He might talk to you if he thought you'd help to protect her from herself."

"What if he's already aiding and abetting?" I said. "She's doing something illegal and he's in on it?"

"In that case," Gabi said, "would you be any worse off than you are now?"

"Swell," I said.

33

Rawlins said he had business in Bel-Air. He asked me to meet him at the hotel. That's all you have to say once you mention the neighborhood. Just 'the hotel.'

I took the I-405 north to Sunset. The Hotel Bel-Air was on Stone Canyon Road, up past the country club. I caught glimpses of new mansions and old sprawling California ranch houses behind eucalyptus trees and palms, stone fences and iron gates.

Gabi had told me that when Bel-Air was built, back in the 1920's, no movie people were allowed to buy houses there. Now, entertainment drove the west L.A. economy. I had no doubt that celebrities were hitting fairways and greens to my left and lolling by their pools to my right, maybe having an afternoon toot to set themselves up for a tough regimen of shopping and lunching.

I pulled into valet parking. My car was two years old and a little dusty, but the valet was unfazed. He gave me directions to the piano bar.

It must have reminded guests of the dens at their English country homes. Paintings of the hunt shared space with impressionists. The chairs matched the dark wood paneling on the walls and had leather seats and backs. I could see myself sitting there for hours, sipping twenty-dollar drinks and chatting with movie stars. Someone had the good sense not to light the fireplace on a day expected to hit ninety-five degrees.

There was a piano, all right, but a poster at the entrance said the pianist played only at night. All I heard was a murmur of quiet conversation from a few customers at the bar.

Rawlins had a table by the side, looking out to the lobby. I laughed as I approached him. Yesterday, I sat in a beer bar off Century Boulevard with a guy whose job description included killing people. Here I was in Bel-Air with a lawyer who owned a helicopter and a Ventura County ranch, wrote for learned journals, and played consort to the Our Lady of the North.

"What's funny?" Rawlins said.

"L.A.," I said.

"I guess," he said. "How about a sherry?"

"Sherry?" I said. "I don't suppose they have Old Milwaukee."

"They have everything here," he said. "If you went in the restaurant and asked for Spaghetti-O's, they'd probably make them from scratch for you. But try the sherry. Maybe it will inspire a civilized discussion."

A waiter had materialized. Rawlins ordered two amontillados without waiting for my choice.

Well, why not? It was his money, and this was just the place for *Jerez* with the z sounding like *th*, and big deals arranged in hushed tones. I pulled my chair close to the table and said, "Lourdes Ortega and her family are safe."

"I'm glad to know that," he said.

"Did you know it already?"

"As long as they're safe, what does that matter?"

"Man, I'd like to get a straight answer from you and Carla sometime," I said. "I'm trying to figure out what happened with these people coming from Mexico, and how it connects to the Liebowitz and Bergstrom murders. And from you, I get questions answered with questions."

"Don't forget, Brinker, you're working for Carla. I have Carla's ear and I have her best interests in mind."

The waiter returned with two small sherry glasses and a plate of the biggest olives west of Andalusia.

Rawlins said, "Look. It's true that I helped her get those people to safety. That's over. It ended well. Your attention now should be on the murder cases. If you don't want to work on those, I think you should refund some of Carla's money. Go chase runaways or peep in motel room windows or whatever you do."

"How did you help with the Ortega family?"

"We went to Nogales. You know that. What we did there was talk to people who consult on certain immigration problems."

"Come on," I said. "You mean people who organize immigrant smuggling."

"Call it whatever you like," he said. "But please knock off the hypocrisy. I got help in Mexico from someone who knows about immigration problems. You get help in Mexico from Hector Ortiz, a known drug boss. You think that's a big secret? It's not, but who cares? We're talking border business, Brinker. Everybody compromises."

"Listen," I said. I was ready to play Gabi's Carla card. "We both know that Carla let something get out of hand with people entering illegally. Even if she did nothing technically wrong, she could get jammed up with the bar association or Homeland Security, or just get some awful press. Why don't you help me to help her?"

He sipped his sherry and looked at me as he mulled an answer.

"You're making some rash assumptions there," he said. "Carla's connection to those people in Phoenix was peripheral at most. And you say the Ortega family is safe, so what exactly is the problem?"

"Who did you see in Nogales?"

"This is irrelevant to your investigation, Brinker."

"Bullshit," I said, careful to keep my voice Bel-Air low. "I'll decide what matters."

"Fine," he said. "You decide what matters to you. I'll decide what's important to Carla and me."

"Do you know Eduardo Salvador?"

"We're done here," Rawlins said.

"I doubt it," I said.

Gabi sat at her kitchen table, a laptop computer open, a phone cradled on her shoulder. She waved as I came in and silently mouthed "blah blah blah." The person on the phone must have been yammering. I got a beer from the fridge and sat across the table from her.

"Thanks very much, Mrs. Newman," she said. "You've been a great help. Yes, in tomorrow morning's paper." She hung up.

"I'm glad you got some useful information," I said. "That's more than I can claim."

"Cheer up, buddy," she said. "It may be your lucky day."

"How so?"

"There was a school bus accident in Sherman Oaks this morning. A few kids got banged up a little, but nothing serious."

"This is lucky for me?"

"I'm making calls for a sidebar story. The bus driver apparently blacked out. A parent called the news desk with a tip. This driver had a heart history. So I'm looking into the health requirements for school bus drivers."

"They must need to have regular medical exams. I hope they do."

"They do," she said.

My interest in school transportation was waning fast. I said, "Why is this my lucky day?"

"Because," Gabi said, "I learned that when bus drivers get physicals, the doctor has to fill out certain forms. The state has a form, or they can use one designed for pilot physicals by the FAA."

"I know this will get interesting soon," I said.

"Stay with me," she said. "Well, that piqued my curiosity. So while I waited for some callbacks, I checked the FAA website. It has all kinds of information about licenses for planes and pilots. It's public. Anybody can look up stuff."

Okay," I said.

"I'm thinking, why don't I look up some famous pilot? I typed in Harrison Ford."

"I'll bet you did," I said."

"I read somewhere that he's a big aviation buff. Turns out that he's licensed to fly anything. Regular planes, seaplanes, helicopters."

"You get his address?" I said.

"Don't worry. He's cute for his age but you have youthful stamina," she said. "But then I thought of Rawlins. So I looked him up, just for fun, and sure enough, there's his license. The FAA calls it a certificate. It says commercial pilot, rotorcraft helicopter."

"I remember he told me that he has a commercial license. It means he can accept money for flying. It's harder to get than a regular private pilot license. David Katz got a commercial license for flying his airplane just to have the extra training."

"Well," Gabi said, "I noticed this listing for date of medical exam. So I did some cross checking, and it turns out that commercial pilots have to have a medical exam once a year. That's more often than private pilots."

"So," I said, "whoopee. Now we know that Rawlins needs a medical exam every year."

"Don't be cranky, sweetie. The thing is, he didn't take his medical exam. It's four months overdue."

"I haven't had a physical this year, either."

"You're not a pilot. Pilots' licenses are no good if the medical exam isn't up to date. So Rawlins is flying illegally."

"Well, I don't think he was going to offer me more rides, anyway."

"You're missing my point," she said. "Why would a guy like that, who's been flying for years and knows the rules, who just bought himself a nice new helicopter, fail to keep his license current?"

It seemed like a dead end discussion. But underestimating Gabi was a serious mistake. Beneath the pretty smile lurked a fiercely determined little terrier who loved to drag information out of its hiding places. So I thought about her question.

"Because," I said, "the physical might have turned up something that he didn't want known?"

"That's what I'm guessing," she said.

"But it's not like a big elaborate test for cancer or some dread disease. They don't have to go to the Mayo Clinic for this."

"No," Gabi said, "but they do have to pee in a cup. And the FAA can order doctors and labs to screen for substances that might render the pilot unfit to operate heavy machinery in the air."

"Uh-oh," I said.

"Exactly what I was thinking," she said.

34

I called David Katz in Tucson to ask about missing medical exams for pilots.

"Interesting if true," he said. "But I would offer two caveats, my boy. First, the FAA's web site may simply be out of date. Remember, this is an agency with an air traffic control system that is roughly twenty years behind the time and nowhere close to adequate for present needs. So public information for casual web surfers may be running a bit late, too."

"Okay," I said.

"The second caveat deals with the absence of a valid medical exam. Let's say your information is correct. And let's say further that this is not simply forgetfulness on the pilot's part. The FAA bans airman use of all manner of otherwise innocent substances. For example, diphenhydramine. Do you know what that is?"

"No," I said.

"You probably have some in your house. It's an ingredient used in many over-the-counter allergy medications. It's banned for pilots because it can make you sleepy. Aviation regulators disfavor sleepy pilots. The point is, Brink, a bad medical is not evidence of cocaine or heroin or any such thing. The man simply may have bought a package of the wrong allergy pills. Or his blood pressure may be up and he's waiting until it improves."

"Swell," I said.

"One more thing," David said. "If he fails to have a physical in one year, his medical certificate is not void. It simply downgrades to the level required for private pilots. That means renewal either two or three years, depending on his age. So your fellow couldn't fly for pay, but he could still fly perfectly legally."

"Too bad," I said. "But the exam could detect an illegal drug?"

"Certainly," David said. "Don't talk up that angle without evidence, though, or I'll be obliged to review my libel law to defend you."

Gabi downloaded a newspaper file photo of Rawlins. She printed two copies for me. The next morning after breakfast, I headed up to the Sunset Strip and José Liebowitz's apartment building.

The door to the small lobby was locked. A tenant directory on the wall had buttons to ring each apartment and a speaker for visitors to announce themselves. A tiny camera above the door was trained on me as I checked the directory. I made a mental note to ask Detective Jansson if there was a videotape record of entries and exits, although it seemed impossible that the cops would have missed that.

I thought about the old movie trick of pressing each button until some tenant expecting pizza buzzed me in. But it was early for pizza, and this building had a recent murder. I doubted that anyone would admit a stranger, even if the camera showed my honest face and kindly manner.

Inside, the elevator door opened. A young man in gray trousers and a blue blazer pushed through the lobby door.

"Excuse me," I said.

He stopped and looked at me without apprehension or irritation.

"I'm investigating Mr. Liebowitz's death," I said. "Have you seen this man around?" I showed him the picture of Rawlins.

"I'm afraid not," he said. "Sorry." He walked up the hill toward Sunset.

The elevator had made another pickup. Two young women in slacks, short-sleeved blouses and high heels smiled at me as they stepped outside. I gave them my most genial "Excuse me," but they kept walking. One said, "Sorry. Late for work."

Nobody else showed for ten minutes. A teenage boy in jeans, plain white T-shirt and a backwards ball cap came out leading an overweight basset hound. The boy just grunted when I approached him. The basset gave a full body wag and tried to check me out. The boy kept walking and yanked on the leash. As he passed, I saw the UCLA logo on the cap. The dog waddled to catch up.

So it went for another hour. Everyone else who exited the building was well fed, well dressed, and poorly informed about other tenants' visitors. A few looked sympathetic when I mentioned Liebowitz. Others sneered.

A fortyish woman, tall with flat shoes, smiled at me as she stepped outside. She wore a silk dress with an abstract red and green pattern. I figured her for a couple of hours at Nordstrom, then lunch with the girls. She lost the smile when I told her why I was there.

"Such a terrible thing to happen to such a nice man," she said. "José lived on my floor. He was always so pleasant. He helped me start my car one morning when I just couldn't manage. And if he ever saw me carrying packages, he always took them and carried them upstairs for me."

I showed her the Rawlins picture.

"Oh, yes," she said. She took the photograph and studied it. "I saw this man going and coming a couple of times from José's apartment. He looked familiar to me, but I couldn't quite place him. Someone who lives nearby, I suppose."

"Did you form any impression of him?" I said. "Was he pleasant or brusque or what?"

"Quiet. Not very communicative," she said. "You can probably tell that I'm a friendly person. I'm always happy to meet people. I start conversations with strangers, especially if they're handsome men a bit younger than myself." She smiled. "One afternoon in the elevator, I said something like 'lovely day.' He just nodded."

"Do you remember when you saw him?" I said.

"Well, not exactly."

"Generally is fine. Months ago? Years ago?"

"Not years, certainly," she said. "I think it was two or three times in the last few weeks before, you know, what happened. Always in the hall as we were coming or going."

I gave her a business card and asked her to call me if she thought of anything else about the man in the picture. She studied the card for a moment.

"Private investigation," she said. "I suppose there's some squalid lawsuit brewing now."

"Not that I know of," I said. "I'm just trying to find out what happened for one of Mr. Liebowitz's former lawyers. She's frustrated that the official investigation seems to be going slowly."

"Well, then, I hope you do find what you need," she said. She took a card from her purse. Her name, Laura M. Collins, was embossed, but there was no other information. She wrote a phone number on the back.

"Call me anytime if you need something more," she said. She gave back the picture, letting her hand brush mine.

I drove along Sunset. I should have been watching my rear view mirror, but it's hard to ignore the scene on the Strip. Sunset is probably what people think all of L.A. is like. I passed a drive-in restaurant with a sign offering valet parking. How does that work, I wondered.

There was a Hustler store, bright and bold with big unembarrassed windows. Smiling, wholesome-looking couples shopped together for porn videos. A big sign read "Love Supplies."

The Whisky a Go Go, a sixties relic, was still there and still in business. This week's acts were listed on the marquee. I hadn't heard of any of them.

The office towers must be crawling with entertainment lawyers and talent agents. I tried to imagine the rental rates for south-facing offices with spectacular views of the L.A. basin. I saw three Ferrari Spiders in five minutes. The racing version could do 196 miles an hour, I heard. These drivers looked content to troll the boulevard slowly, catching smiles from pretty girls wearing small dresses in sidewalk cafes.

So. Richard Rawlins, my outwardly helpful and good-humored pilot who lately turned irritable and secretive, lied to me. He said he had met José Liebowitz and Bo Bergstrom casually at parties, or maybe in Carla's office. But I believed that Laura M. Collins could accurately identify a wealthy lawyer at two-hundred yards in pitch darkness, let alone up close in her own hallway.

Gotcha, Rich.

I just don't know what I gotcha at.

I had Jansson's number on my cell phone. He picked up on the first ring.

"You knew there was a camera over José Liebowitz's lobby door, right?" I said.

"Not only that," he said, "I know it's live only. No videotape, dammit. We could've had some creep halfway to the green room in San Quentin by now if we got pictures."

"Just thought I'd ask," I said.

"What are you doing at the building?" Jansson said.

He had been pretty forthcoming with me, but I wasn't ready to drop the name of Richard Rawlins.

"Just canvassing the neighbors," I said.

"We did that. Any joy?"

"Nope," I said.

"Me, neither. You'll let me know if you get some, right?"

"Absolutely." "Okay," he said. "Give Carla a pat on the ass for me."

"Oh, right," I said. I hung up.

The glamour falls away fast as Sunset descends toward Hollywood. Somewhere east of Fairfax, the Ferraris and finery dissolve to strip malls and delivery trucks, to threadbare apartment buildings and a hardscrabble street life. I doubt that anybody there even bothers to dream of steady work, let alone stardom.

So profound was the change of landscape that I had forgotten where I was going. I could take Sunset all the way downtown or jump on the Hollywood Freeway. It was early for rush hour, so I decided to chance the freeway.

As I passed Van Ness and headed down the onramp, I looked in the rear view mirror. A late model Ford sedan skidded around another car, cut across the right lane, and raced down the ramp behind me. Two young guys were in the front seats. They looked familiar, maybe from Dodger Stadium.

The driver seemed to know that he screwed up. He slowed down and let two cars pass him. One turned off at the Western Avenue exit. The other bailed out at Melrose. Once again, the Ford driver eased up and let another car get between us.

Amateur hour. Good to know.

I took the 110 at downtown and got off at Sixth Street. I wound through the crowded city blocks and found the entrance to Carla's office building garage. After I parked and boarded the elevator, I pressed the buttons for the lobby and for Carla's floor. As the doors opened, there was one of the guys from the Ford, staring in the building's front window. His eyes met mine. Before he could look away, I winked. He looked angry as the doors closed and the elevator took me up to seventeen and Carla.

35

Amric led me into the office. Carla sat behind her desk. Her hair was rumpled. Her eyes were puffy. She didn't look like our lady of anything.

Amric said, "I'm so sorry about the picture, Mr. Brinker. The oversight was my fault entirely."

I nodded. Carla said, "I didn't know the guy, anyway. No harm done, Amric."

"Well, I do apologize," Amric said. He backed out of the office, almost bowing, and closed the door.

"Rich thinks we should pay you off and send you home," Carla said.

"I'll bet," I said.

"I'm inclined to agree with him," Carla said. "The Ortegas are safe, and I thank you for confirming that for me. It was worth your entire fee, actually, so I'm not looking for any money back. But there's really nothing you can do about José or Bo that the police can't do. I expected too much on that. So I've decided to terminate your obligation."

I pulled up the client chair and sat down across the desk from her.

"Okay, Carla. You can fire me. But I won't quit the case no matter what you do."

"Oh, come on, Brinker," she said, struggling to sound amused. "That's silly macho talk. You don't stay on a case when you have no client."

"I haven't worked off your ten grand yet," I said. "But that's not it. The men who started tailing me when this whole mess began are back at it. They're downstairs, waiting for me come out. Somebody tried to break into Gabi's apartment. I can handle a few second rate hoods following me around, but the rules change if they mess with Gabi."

"I understand that completely," Carla said.

"And I have new facts about José Liebowitz that the cops don't have. They might shed some light on his murder. I can't walk away from that. So you do whatever you want, but I'm in this to the end."

Her eyes regained a bit of brightness when I mentioned Liebowitz.

"What's the new information about José?" Carla asked.

"I can't tell you yet," I said.

"What do you mean, you can't tell me?" A bit of the zealous advocate had stepped tentatively back into action.

"You just fired me," I said.

Her expression registered not anger, but disappointment. I had let her down. That look had made many a man change his mind, I'll bet, and beg her forgiveness in return for a smile.

"Let me ask you something, Carla," I said. "Did you and José ever have anything going, personally?"

"Anything going?" she said. "You mean romantically?"

"Yes."

"No," she said, but her voice was hesitant, not emphatic. She looked away as she spoke.

Give her a minute, I thought. The air conditioner droned, barely audible in Carla's insulated office. Telephones in other rooms rang softly and were answered immediately. Voices with many accents rose and fell in the hall as people moved about. Small, broken clouds drifted over downtown. Through tinted glass, they dimmed the room's natural light almost imperceptibly.

Carla said very softly, "Why would you ask me that?"

I shook my head. "Tell me about it, Carla."

For a moment, I thought she was struggling to breathe. But she straightened in her chair and looked directly at me.

"I hate to disappoint people. I hate to fail. I hate not being everything I'm supposed to be. I hate saying no."

I waited as she calculated how far to go with this.

She said, "Do you remember me from Tucson?"

"Sure," I said. "All us guys remember you."

She laughed without joy. "Then maybe you'll understand what I mean by this. I feel like such an idiot, such a snob. I've always hated to say no, but certain girls have to learn early how to do that. And I mean girls, not women. Kids. I had to learn."

"The girls all the guys had crushes on," I said.

"Yes. And the way you say no with kindness in that situation is to absolve the guy of failure. You're wonderful, but I'm not good enough. Or I'm not ready. Or I have a boyfriend back in New Mexico, even though I didn't. I knew I was causing pain, but I would try not to make it humiliating, too."

"Plenty of pain to go around in high school," I said.

"José had a crush on me," she said. "It sounds odd to say 'crush' when you're talking about a perfectly mature adult, but that's what it was. I'd finish a project for him and he'd send me flowers with the check. We'd have meetings and he'd always try to arrange them right at midday so he could ask me to lunch, or at five o'clock so he could ask me to have drinks or dinner. It was perfectly proper, nothing untoward or obnoxious. I certainly never felt afraid. It was just like having a little puppy nipping at my ankles all the time."

"How did you say no to him?" I said. "How did you handle the letdown?"

"I told him that I was already with someone," she said. "And he said, 'That's okay. I'll be around.' He never made another move, but it was clear that he was available if ever I was."

"What about Bo Bergstrom?" I said.

Carla closed her eyes and looked down. She took a tissue from a box on her desk.

"A wonderful man," she said. "I think I told you that when you first came here."

"Yes, you did."

"Early in the spring, he realized that the farm would need much more help than usual this year. Bo's Berries had bought some adjoining property, so there was more land to work. The weather looked promising for a heavy harvest later in the year. The Bergstroms wouldn't just go down to some parking lot and hire workers out of a truck. Everybody had to be properly documented, legally in the country, work permits, and all."

"So you found yourself spending extra time with him."

"Yes. At first, he'd come here, like any client comes to his lawyer's office. Occasionally, I'd go up there, especially if papers needed filing at the courthouse in Ventura. Then I found myself looking for excuses to leave here and go up to Camarillo. We'd work late. Do I have to draw a picture for you?"

"No," I said.

"I don't know how serious it was with Bo," she said, "but it wasn't just some fling. He was such a solid guy, self-confident but not full of himself. Maybe farmers are that way. They battle nature all their lives, so other problems don't seem too big. Here in L.A., every person's problems are a big deal, like they never happened to anyone else. Bo just took things in stride."

"How did Rawlins feel about this?" I asked.

"Rich? Well, I wasn't exactly reporting to him about Bo."

"But he must have sensed some change in your relationship with him."

"There was no change in the existing relationship," Carla said. "Oh, I broke a dinner date with Rich one night when I decided to stay in Camarillo. But Rich has always understood that I'm my own person. If anyone tries to control me, he understands that it will have just the opposite effect."

"He might have known those things," I said. "I wonder if he understood them."

She regarded me carefully, looking as though she had just made an unpleasant discovery. I suspected that the vulnerable woman had stepped aside and let the lawyer go back to work.

"I want to know why you're asking me these questions," she said.

"You're the common thread, Carla. You're the only person who acknowledges knowing both those men."

"My God, Brinker," she said. "You can't possibly be suggesting that I killed those men. I'm the last person who would wish them any harm."

"I don't suspect you, Carla," I said.

"Well, then, good luck in doing what two police agencies can't. Goodbye, Brinker."

Amric, his service impeccably timed and silent as always, was holding the door open as I rose to leave.

36

I drove up the ramp from Carla's garage. The Ford was on the street, waiting. It pulled out of an empty bus stop across the street and settled into traffic a couple of cars behind me.

Downtown tails are tough. There's a light every block. If the light changes to red and either of the two drivers between the tail and me decides to stop, it's over. My followers knew I made them before, so they had to risk it, staying back out of sight.

That was their problem. My problem was finding a way to let them stay close until I had them where I wanted them.

I worked my way over to Wilshire Boulevard and drove northwest. I kept it slow and watched the traffic lights two blocks ahead. I never got too far in front of my followers to leave them stuck at a red.

MacArthur Park had plenty of places for what I wanted, but I remembered the LAPD substation at Wilshire and Alvarado. Gabi told me that cops always cruised around the park, looking for gangbangers and drug dealers. It had been a violent crime capital for many years. When they drained the lake for the subway project, they supposedly found hundreds of discarded guns lying on the bottom. Neighborhood groups and businesses forced a cleanup. Now the cops kept it safe with heavy visibility of cars and uniforms. No good.

Wilshire curved at Lafayette Park and headed due west. My tail was still with me. On the left, I saw the old Bullocks Wilshire department store's art deco tower. The store closed years ago and Southwestern Law School restored it. Gabi had talked about going to law school and Southwestern was on her list of possibilities. I remembered the big parking lot behind the building. It would have plenty of places open on this late summer afternoon.

There was no left turn from Wilshire, so I pressed on to Vermont and joined the crowd in the turn lane. It looked good. I was third in line. The followers had left just one car between us. They would certainly make the same light that I did. The left turners started moving and the tail car swung through the intersection easily. I drove the short distance to Seventh, took another left, then made the final turns into Wilshire Place and the entrance to Southwestern's parking lot.

It was summer, but the parking kiosk was open. I took a ticket and drove around to the covered parking level. The tails would not want to get stuck inside, I figured. Sure enough, no car followed me. They would stay on the street and wait for me to leave through the same gate.

I parked as close as possible to the rear of the old Bullocks, locked the car, and headed into the building. Once inside, I walked through the grand old hall to the front. A few students sat in beautiful period furniture reupholstered with alumni dollars. They ignored me. Finally, an advantage to being over thirty.

I came out under the tower on Wilshire Boulevard. I walked east and peered around the corner, looking south on Wilshire Place. Sure enough, there was the Ford, parked just north of the entrance, its rear end facing me. Predictable. Perfect.

The two men in the front seat watched the kiosk where I had entered the parking lot. They didn't talk to each other. The driver's window was down, probably to let the faint breeze cool the car without running the air conditioning. When I approached, it would have to be from left rear, and quietly.

I looked around. The law school must be a low crime area. Not a cop car was in sight. This being Los Angeles, there was no danger of foot patrols. I wore a lightweight blue blazer that looked right at home in lawyerland and nicely covered my shoulder rig. I put my hand inside the jacket and stepped quickly across Westmoreland to the opposite sidewalk. I could walk close to the north-facing cars and stay clear of my tails' rear view mirror.

They never saw me coming.

I stuck my gun through the driver's open window and said, "*Hola*, guys."

They looked at me, but mainly they looked at the gun.

"Shit," the passenger said.

I scanned the front seat area and the two men. They had no weapon that I could see.

"You guys still aren't carrying since your two pals got shot over by the copy shop?" I said.

"We're not killers like your friend Delgado," the driver said.

"He's not my friend," I said.

"Sure," the driver said. "But we got orders just to watch. We're not gonna make you no trouble."

He was the jerk who had picked me up at Carla's office and followed me to Dodger Stadium.

"I'm lowering the gun so it won't bother anybody walking by," I said. "I can have it back in your face in a heartbeat. Raise it and pull the trigger in one move."

"Relax," the driver said.

"Your description matches the amateur who tried to break into an apartment at Marina del Rey," I said.

"That was nothing, man," he said. "I waited until your girl friend left for the day. Even if she came back, like that other bitch with the cold, I wouldn't have touched her. I'd have just left."

"What were you looking for?"

"Why don't you put that gun away?" the passenger said. "Make me nervous, standing there with a damn gun. We got two friends shot already for no good reason."

"So give me a good reason not to shoot you," I said. "One more time. What were you looking for?"

"Just papers, man. Any papers about immigration or some murder cases. If there was a laptop lying around, I should take that, too."

"Who sent you?"

"Guy we work for," the driver said. He raised his chin and toughened his tone. "I'm not gonna tell you his name. He'd kill us. I don't think you will. Even if you would, he'd kill us worse, you know what I mean?"

I put the gun right up to his ear.

"Anyway," the man said, "he got the job from somebody else. I don't know who that was."

"Two down already," I said. "Why make it four?"

The passenger believed it. He said, "Jeez, Chuy, tell him something."

Chuy said, "Do what you gotta do, man. But I don't think you're gonna shoot us. Not in broad daylight, anyway. Get blood on your nice jacket. Somebody could walk out of that building any second. Anyway, I don't think you're gonna do it."

I stepped back but pointed the pistol toward the car window.

"You're going to drive away from here," I said. "You're going to tell your boss that he'll be out of hired help if this keeps up. If I catch you following me again, you get hurt. If I see you anywhere near that marina apartment or the woman who lives there, I'll kill you both. *¿Entienden?*"

"Yeah, we get it," Chuy said. He turned the key in the ignition and the engine started. I lowered my gun.

"Might not be us you should look for now," he said, then he drove carefully down to Seventh Street. He turned right and I watched him drive out of sight.

I was bluffing when I said I would kill them both. But as I thought of Gabi, dragged into another mess of my making, the threat felt real.

37

In the middle east, always hot enough to blow up, the searing desert wind is called the levanter. In Southern California, it's the Santa Ana. Typically it arrives in the fall. That year it blew in early. "Preview of coming attractions," the TV weather forecasters joked, but it was not funny to firefighters. Santa Ana winds could hit thirty to forty miles an hour, pushing temperatures up to the hundreds and humidity down to nothing.

Gabi said, "I think I'll be on fire duty for a while. They lost five more homes in La Habra Heights yesterday. The Santa Ana's making it worse. The paper's pouring extra people into the coverage."

"Be careful out there," I said. "Remember Summerhaven."

Summerhaven is a getaway town in the Catalina Mountains north of Tucson. It was virtually leveled by a fast moving, direction-switching fire a few years earlier. Tucsonans thought of that one as The Fire. We didn't realize the Southern Californians face the same threat every year.

"You be careful right here," Gabi said. "I read a book once that called heat like this 'bread knife weather' because it makes people crazy. They get out the bread knives and start slashing each other."

We were inside her apartment with the air conditioning on. Fresh breezes off the ocean usually cooled the place. Now the wind came from the east, rolling down the mountains, gathering heat as it moved, and blow-drying the basin.

My cell phone rang. It was Jansson.

"You'll never guess," he said. "Phoenix P.D. put out a want on Eduardo Salvador. I flagged it to call me in case he showed up here. Lo and behold, a busted tail light at Melrose and Robertson. Escalade with Colorado plates. An alert deputy, as we say, brought him in. Phoenix is coming to pick him up, but I get first crack. You want to take a run on the Liebowitz thing?"

"Just say when," I said.

"One hour, West Hollywood station," Jansson said.

Eduardo Salvador was in an interrogation room. A uniformed deputy stood outside the door. Salvador was a solid, compact man, short and muscular. He wore an expensive looking Hawaiian shirt. His ankles were chained. His hands were cuffed. He sat at an old Formica table, looking bored but not nervous. I walked across the room and leaned against the wall.

Jansson sat opposite Salvador. He turned on a tape recorder, identified himself but said nothing about me, then read the Miranda warning. He gave Salvador an acknowledgement form to sign. Salvador signed it, despite his cuffed hands, and pushed it back.

"Mister Salvador," Jansson said, "do you understand why you're being detained?"

"Broken tail light," Salvador said. "I gotta tell you, leg irons and all seem a little harsh. I could get the light fixed this afternoon."

It was the kind of wiseass remark that plenty of cops would answer with a punch in the nose. Jansson stayed cool and kept his polite tone.

"Actually, Mister Salvador, you're being held on a warrant from Phoenix, Arizona. You're wanted for questioning in four to eight murders."

"Okay," Salvador said.

"Okay what?" Jansson said.

"Okay, I'll listen to their questions."

"Before that," Jansson said, "I have some questions for you concerning a case here in Los Angeles County. Do you or did you ever know a man named Joseph or José Liebowitz?"

"No."

"Do you or did you ever know his attorney, Carla Baca?"

"I've heard of her. Immigration babe, right?"

"Probably not how she'd put it, but yeah. You don't know her personally?"

"No."

"Can you account for your presence on the night of May fourteenth, this year?"

"No."

"Why not?" Jansson asked.

"Can you account for yours?" Salvador said. "I was at home in Denver around the middle of May, but I don't keep track of every day."

"What's your business?"

"International consulting."

"You must do pretty well," Jansson said. "That's a nice car. Expensive."

Salvador shrugged.

"What kind of international consulting?" the detective asked.

"Goods and services," Salvador said.

"Who are your clients?"

"Business with international dealings."

Jansson said, "It would help, Mister Salvador, if you were a little more forthcoming."

"Help who?" Salvador said. "Look, I confess to the tail light. That's it for now. If cops are coming from Phoenix to extradite me, I want to call my lawyer."

Jansson looked at me. I nodded. He said, "We are now terminating this interview," and gave the time. He switched off the recorder and removed the cassette. He left the room and slammed the door behind him.

Salvador looked across the room and regarded me.

"You're the one who slaps me around while the tape is stopped and the other cops are outside, I suppose," he said.

"Not me," I said. "I'm not even a cop. Besides, I owe you."

"Sure," he said. "You're my best pal."

I walked over to the table and sat down.

"I know who you are," he said. "You're a private eye from Tucson. You're in way over your head. You have no idea."

"How do you know who I am?" I asked.

He just smiled.

"I have an idea who your best friends are," I said. "Lourdes Ortega. And Pablo Ortega and little Irma."

He was good. His expression remained impassive. His breathing was regular. He did not avert his eyes.

He said, "Means nothing to me."

"The house in Phoenix where you found them," I said. "Four dead in that house. Four more out on the res. The Phoenix cops like you for all of them. And the feds are in because of illegal immigration and the bodies on reservation land. But Lourdes and her family were there. They didn't see you do anything wrong. You got them out of there."

"Are they going to get me out of here?" he said.

"If you don't get helpful, you could be in a cell somewhere for the rest of your life. Or there'll be a hot shot waiting for you."

Salvador shook his head.

"You guys are all alike," he said. "You think every Latino you meet just fell off a watermelon truck in Yuma. There is nothing, absolutely nothing, to put me together with whatever happened in that house."

"Dulce," I said, looking him hard in the eyes.

"Dulce," he said, giving the look right back. "Sweet."

"I'm wondering what kind of man you are," I said. "You let a whole family go, even though they could tie you to multiple murders. You let Dulce go, too. But you raped her."

"I never raped anybody," he said. "No Dulce is going to say I did."

I leaned in close, getting my face only a few inches from his.

"I need to know why you were at that house," I said. "Who sent you? What were your orders?"

Salvador leaned back and smiled.

"Your sheriff friend has nothing on me for his murder case. You've got nothing on me for yours. Maybe you and I could have a talk sometime when I get the handcuffs and leg chain off, and I'm walking around in the sunshine. For now, fuck off."

"The Phoenix cops can't wait to get you back there," I said.

"*Idiotas*," he said. "I'll call my lawyer now."

Jansson said, "I've got nothing to hold him on except the Phoenix warrant. Maybe somebody can put him in that murder house, but nothing links him with Liebowitz."

"What happens next?" I said.

"We'll take him down to central jail to hold him overnight. The Phoenix people will be here tomorrow. They'll partner up with the local D.A.'s office for the extradition hearing. His lawyer will try to quash the warrant. I think he can do it, too. All they've got is a cop who saw Salvador eating fast food near the crime scene. The cops must have had a friendly judge in Arizona, but it's gonna be a hard sell here."

"So if extradition fails, then he walks?"

"Out the door," Jansson said, "showing us his middle finger."

"I don't see him for Liebowitz," I said.

"Me, neither," Jansson said. "Isn't law enforcement fulfilling?"

38

Gabi found Dulce.

I had brought dinner, sandwiches that I picked up at a deli near the marina. I wanted to tell her about my confrontations with the guys tailing me, and about the cop shop talk with Eduardo Salvador. Before I could say a word, she told me her news.

"I called Fidelia to thank her for helping us with the Ortega family," Gabi said. "She said, 'There's someone else you should meet if your Mister Brinker wants to know what really happened in Phoenix. Her name is Dulce.' I about jumped out of my skin. I said, '*Abuela*, when we can we see her?' Fidelia said Dulce will never speak to a man about what happened, but if I come, she'll talk to me."

"You went today?"

"You bet. I tried to call you but your cell must have been off."

"I was at the sheriff's station. I'll tell you about it later. Go on."

"Dulce has a job already. You remember that she stayed in the van when the Ortegas got off in Redlands. She came to East L.A. and Fidelia's little underground took over. They say she's working at a house in Los Feliz. Housekeeper and nanny. They brought her to Diego's place near Fidelia's to meet me."

"No cutouts and hideouts?"

"Fidelia trusts us both," Gabi said.

"So," I said. I took the sandwiches and Dr. Brown sodas out of the bag. Gabi took hers but she was too wound up to eat or drink yet.

"So, we sat down for an hour. Dulce's a pretty girl. Young face, lush figure. You can see why some depraved asshole like Salvador would go after her."

"It was Salvador, then?"

"No doubt whatsoever. I had his picture. When I showed it to her, I thought she was going to be sick. It was all she could do not to spit on it."

I unwrapped my sandwich and began to eat. Gabi picked up her notebook and studied it for a moment.

"There were five of them, plus Lourdes Ortega's baby. The *coyotes* put them all in one room. The people didn't know why because the house had other bedrooms. They figured those rooms must be saved for other groups of immigrants coming through."

"Probably," I said. "That whole block was scheduled for demolition. It might have been the only house that still had water and power. The only place to hide them for layovers."

"The deal was, a new crew would pick them up in Phoenix and take them to California. The two guys were going to Blythe. Lourdes and her family and Dulce were going to L.A."

"But the Ortega family wound up in Redlands. I think it's because José Liebowitz's sister was nearby in Riverside. She could take care of them temporarily. She has some connection with Fidelia to help people."

Gabi popped the tab on a cream soda and took a sip.

"Here's the thing," she said. "When Salvador and his crew showed up, there was a big commotion and some shooting. Dulce doesn't know what happened exactly, because she was in locked in another bedroom by herself. But she knows there was trouble. And she never saw her original *coyotes* again."

I leaned and closed my eyes. I rubbed my temples. I drank some soda and ran the side of the cool can across my forehead. Anything to get this mess into focus.

"Maybe Salvador hijacked that job," I said. "He wasn't part of the original smuggling crew. He just came and took over. He killed the guys who got in the way. Vicente told me it goes down that way sometimes."

"Maybe," Gabi said.

"But the Ortegas didn't say anything about getting shaken down," I said. "That's what usually happens. The new *coyotes* tell the people, 'Okay, you paid them. We just replaced them. Now you have to pay us.' But Lourdes and Pablo weren't held up like that."

"Neither was Dulce," Gabi said. "She was robbed another way."

"You better tell me about that," I said.

"After the ruckus, Salvador came into the room and locked the door behind him. He said he was in charge now, and she had to be nice to him. She said no. He could beat her up or kill her, for that matter, but she wouldn't. And he said, 'I'm not going to hurt you. No, not at all. I'm going to go see your friend in the other room. I'll beat her, and she won't be the only one in pain, will she? Her husband will get to watch, and her little girl. And there's another child to think about. So you decide, sweet thing.' Dear God, Brink. Can you believe that?"

"Yes," I said. "I hate to, but I can."

"So," Gabi said, "Dulce stood there in front of this animal, and took off her clothes, and lay down on the bed, and let him. You want me to tell you everything he did, and made her do?"

"No," I said. "I already know enough."

The room felt close. The silence was awkward, even for Gabi and me. I opened the sliding door to the balcony. The breeze and the sounds of the marina spilled in. Happy young people laughed on the boat decks and café patios.

"Fidelia said Dulce was torn up by guilt. Like, she was responsible for what happened. She thought she sinned because she gave in. Fidelia got a priest to come in and counsel her. He said what happened to her was rape. No question in the law or the eyes of God. No different than if the guy had overpowered her physically. He said she sacrificed herself to save a whole family from something truly evil, and that was no sin. The message is getting through, apparently, but it's tough."

We sat there, neither of us eating or drinking. I was wondering what I would have been done to Salvador, alone in that interrogation room, if I had known this a few hours earlier.

"But why didn't he rob the rest of them?" I said. "We know he's total scum. No morals at all. Why was he unspeakably vicious to her and not to them?"

"A sociopath who thinks with his dick," Gabi said. "Wouldn't be the first guy like that."

I shook my head. "No, that's not it. I've met him, don't forget. I agree that he's a creep, but mainly he's a professional criminal. He thinks about what he does and what he says."

"He's sick," Gabi said. "He raped that sweet young girl because he could."

"That's it," I said. "He didn't harm the Ortegas because he couldn't. He was there to make sure that they got through safely."

I could see Gabi putting it together. She already was sad and angry, but now her expression darkened even more.

"If that's true," she said, "he forced Dulce with a lie. He couldn't touch Lourdes."

"And who would have hired him to protect the Oretgas and bring them here?" I said.

"A lawyer who sent a letter practically inviting her to come here illegally," Gabi said.

"No," I said. "Not Carla. Someone who knew Carla sent that letter. Someone who wants to keep Carla from harm."

39

Vicente answered on the first ring.

"Where are you?" I said.

"Home in Nogales. You still in L.A.?"

"Yeah. Can you talk?"

"Let me call you back on a clean phone," he said. "Got one in the next room."

I hung up. Vicente and Hector kept a stock of throwaway cell phones with prepaid time. If a phone ever got traced, it would lead to a fake name and a trash dump somewhere in Sonora. Vicente called back in thirty seconds.

"Salvador," I said. "If someone here wanted to hire him, would they come to you or a somebody like you in Nogales?"

"Somebody like me? You mean brave, intelligent, irresistible to women?"

"Like your company," I said.

"Not us," Vicente said. "We don't deal with him. But you could find him through brokers here, or Juárez, or Tijuana. Lots of places."

"Nogales," I said. "Who in Nogales?"

"Whoa," he said. "Above my pay grade. Hold on a minute."

I heard muffled conversation in the background. Finally, Hector came on the line.

"Why do you want to know this?" he said.

"Because somebody there put Salvador on the road to that house in Phoenix," I said. "Salvador killed a bunch of people and raped a girl, but let a protected family go. I need to know who set that up. I need to know who paid, and how, and when."

Hector said, "What are you going to do if I give you a name? Come down and interrogate this person? Have a nice, what do you call it, a nice deposition where everybody answers questions under oath and shakes hands at the end? Maybe have a drink after?"

"Maybe not the nice part," I said.

"Sure," Hector said. "And you're going to pitch to A-Rod and strike him out with three fast balls. Brinker, sometimes I think you're the dumbest gringo in the whole damn country. Either damn country."

"I need these answers. I'm coming down there."

"No, you're not. Here's how I know. My guys are watching. If you come across the line, they're going to pick you up and bring you here. We'll lock you in a room until this stupid idea wears off. I'll send in Frida and María if you want. But you're not going to butt heads with some asshole who'd rather kill you than talk to you."

"You have a better idea?" I said.

"Yeah, I do," Hector said. "You'll get your answer. But don't call me, *hermano*. I'll call you."

The line went dead.

Amric, on the phone, said, "Perhaps I should not be talking to you any longer, Mr. Brinker."

"A quick question, Amric," I said. "When Carla sent that letter to Lourdes Ortega, who knew about it?"

He did not answer although he had all the answers. I knew that he was sorting out the implications of telling me.

"Myself, of course," he said.

"Who else? What about Terry O'Laughlin?"

"He would have no reason to know unless Carla told him," Amric said. "Of course, he does have access to all our computers, so he might have found the letter by chance. We have never had any reason to think that Mr. O'Laughlin abuses the privilege."

"Yet," I said.

"*Abuela*," I said, "do you know Carla Baca?"

Fidelia Ramos sat in the same big chair in her living room. She kept an eye on the street, although it was dark now and nothing moved in the quiet neighborhood. Gabi was at my side. Fidelia's son Diego sat across the room, looking as stern as the young Marine in the photograph.

"Of course," Fidelia said. "Carla helps people in her way, and I help them in mine."

"Do you help together sometimes?"

She sipped her coffee and made a face.

"Decaf," she said. "Terrible, but nobody has brought me any real coffee from Mexico yet. I wish I could send Diego to Oaxaca or Chiapas to buy some, but that would be so extravagant."

I smiled. Gabi smiled. Diego was not smiling.

We waited. Fidelia leaned over to put her coffee cup on a saucer on the table beside her chair. The motion seemed to tax her strength.

"I'm glad you don't hurry me, Mister Brinker, although you're so anxious to know," the old woman said. "I appreciate that. Young people always want to go, go, go. Old people like me need a moment to think."

I nodded and gave what I hoped was a grateful smile.

"Now that I've thought," Fidelia said, "let me save us time so I can go to bed. You want to know if I cooperated with Carla in bringing the Ortegas here. The answer is partly yes. I knew nothing about them before they came across the border. Carla called me and asked if I could find a safe place for them in California if she could get them here from Arizona. I said I could. You know Sandra Brown? Sandra Liebowitz Brown, it is. She has helped me in this way before. She's wonderful with families and especially little children. Does this answer your question?"

"If you can tell me, *abuela*," I said, "I need to know one more thing."

"Just one," Diego said sharply from across the small room.

I leaned closer to Fidelia and said, "You had to tell someone how to find Sandra Brown and deliver the Ortega family safely. Who was that and what was your contact with him?"

Diego said, "Mamá."

"No, Diego," she said. "I told Mister Brinker that I would answer his questions. I will. Carla gave us a number so we could call without revealing any more information than necessary. The man's name was Eduardo, she said. We called and told him where to bring the Ortegas. We made it clear that they were to be protected. Carla had arranged to pay for his services. I gather she had put some money down with the balance to be paid once the Ortegas were safe."

"Eduardo," I said.

"*¡Bastante!*" Diego said. Enough.

Fidelia held up a hand to her son.

"Diego," she said, "there must be no confusion here. People must always know that we try to do the right thing. Mister Brinker, you know that this man is Eduardo Salvador. And you know that I have heard Dulce's story. I'm an old woman. This was not the first mistake I have made. But it may be the worst. The very worst."

She sat up a little straighter, I thought, and there was less kindness in her voice. "This man Salvador betrayed me. He killed many people, or caused their deaths, and he violated an innocent girl. Carla was careless, but she meant well. I forgive a good person's error as my savior Jesucristo would forgive me, I believe."

She spoke Christ's name in the Spanish way. I could picture her in a little Mexican church, her head covered with a lace mantilla, praying for guidance to choose the proper path.

"I am not so Christian about betrayal," she said in such a soft sleepy voice that we barely heard her. "God help me." She closed her eyes.

Diego showed us out. The Dobermans stood at his side and watched us go.

40

Gabi was supposed to have the day off. Her editor called while we ate breakfast. She listened. She hung up looking miserable.

"Back to the fire," she said. "The firefighters are really nervous about the wind for the next couple of days. It keeps gusting on them. They're afraid some of their people might get trapped in flare-ups. I'll try to get home tonight, but he said I might have to stay there for a while. That means sixteen hour days and some crappy motel by myself."

"I'll come out there," I said.

"I'll be too tired for conjugal visits," she said. "Hell, I'll be too tired for phone sex. But I'll call you anyway."

"We gotta get out of this place," I said.

"Eric Burdon and The Animals, 1965," Gabi said. "Wouldn't it be great? Just for a day. No brush fires, no killings."

"Is there such a place in Southern California?"

"Sure," she said. "But it's a different place every day."

She went off to pack a few things. I thought about the cases that brought me here. It was clear that Salvador was behind the murders in Phoenix. Someone sent him there, but did he kill at that someone's orders or on his own? I still had nothing solid about José Liebowitz and Bo Bergstrom. Just a suspicion of Richard Rawlins and uneasy feelings about Terry O'Laughlin.

Gabi came back with a big bag slung over her shoulder and car keys in her hand. I stood up for a hug and a kiss.

"Can I borrow your library card?" I said.

She dug her purse out of the big bag and dug her card out of the purse. She gave it to me and kissed me again.

"*Hasta* whenever," she said.

I finished the coffee and did the breakfast dishes. I read the paper. I thought about Carla Baca and Richard Rawlins and the unknowable dynamic of their relationship. I turned on the television, but it was all commercials and B-list celebrities plugging something useless. I wondered about hoods tailing me and other hoods tailing them. I tried to imagine what sweet little old Fidelia Ramos did when she felt un-Christian.

At eleven o'clock I walked past the boat docks and down to the county library on Admiralty Way. Most of the morning crowd looked to be young moms and little kids arriving for story time. I had my choice of computer terminals in the grownup section. Gabi's card gave me a login ID. She had her password taped on the back of the card. Great security, girl. What would Terry O'Laughlin say about that?

I logged onto the magazine index and ran a search using "Carla Baca" and "Richard Rawlins." No hits. That was a pretty good indication that magazines had never written about them in the same article. I tried the newspaper index and the freestanding L.A. Times index. Same result. Whatever their relationship, Carla and Rawlins had managed to keep it out of the celeb crazed media.

While I was in the Times archives, I ran searches on José Liebowitz and Bo Bergstrom. There was one story on Bergstrom, a just-the-facts piece that ran the day after his body was found. Liebowitz rated a few more items. A reporter had followed up twice with Jansson. The detective said several leads were being pursued. Right. The last mention was in a music review. One of José's clients, a tenor from Mexico City, had dedicated a song to him during a concert at UCLA.

I went back to the newspaper index and tried "Rawlins, Richard." That produced hundreds of hits, mainly online directory listings for people named Richard Rawlins all over the country. I added "Los Angeles." The screen showed several listings for the Rawlins law firm.

One entry jumped out at me. It was a case locator site for the Eighth Judicial District Court, Clark County, Nevada. Las Vegas. Rawlins, Richard of Los Angeles, California had been charged eleven months earlier with violating Nevada Revised Statute section 484.3795, to wit, operating a motor vehicle under the combined influence of alcohol and a controlled substance, cocaine in an amount exceeding 100 blood nanograms per milliliter.

Oh, Gabi, I thought. You clever angel, you. She takes hunches and looks for ways to prove them. I look for ways to dismiss them. I had blown off her excursion into the minutiae of pilot licensing, but now I bet she nailed it. Rawlins skipped his pilot medical exam because he might have had drugs in his system. Did Carla know? Did Rawlins supply cocaine to José Liebowitz?

I followed the links on the court site. Rawlins somehow pleaded the charges down to careless driving. I guessed that he had a good Vegas lawyer and blood tests that barely bumped him into the violation category. A cocaine conviction could have led to disbarment, but a careless driving plea might not even have to be reported to the California Bar.

Nice job working the system, Rich. But it's a new world. What happens in Vegas stays on some server forever.

The library computer timed me out. I signed off and walked back to the apartment. Hector called as I stood on the balcony watching the sailboats come and go.

"Salvador was hired by a man named Rafael Castillo. He's what I would call a business rival in Nogales. A very bad guy. Ordinarily I wouldn't trust a word he says. But I think he was being honest today."

"Why?" I asked.

"Vicente's persuasive powers," Hector said. "Castillo claims that a man from California came here to Nogales and asked if any immigrants from Guaymas were being taken to California. Castillo knows these things because he uses immigrants to clear the way for drug shipments. I tried to explain this when you were here before."

"The immigrants are taken ahead to be sure the Border Patrol or the DEA isn't working that route," I said.

"Exactly. If the immigrants get caught, tough shit. If they make it through, the drug shipments come right behind them."

"Nice business, Hector."

"Well, as one of your statesmen said, we go to war with the army we have. Immigrants are the biggest army on the border, and the most expendable."

"So," I said, "this Californian hires Castillo, and Castillo brings in Salvador?"

"That's right. The guy gave Castillo a name. Ortega. A couple with a child. The job was to get those people to Los Angeles. Later, the guy called and gave an address in Redlands. It's about an hour east of L.A."

"I know where it is."

"Okay," Hector said. "Castillo asked what about the other *pollos* with this family. The guy said he didn't care, but the Ortegas had to be protected absolutely. Castillo says, we can do that. He looks this guy up and down and figures there's some money talking. He says twenty-thousand dollars. The guy pulls out ten-thousand, American cash, and says he'll bring the other half when the goods are delivered. Castillo figures, shit, I made a profit already, so he says okay."

"Let me guess something," I said. "When the guy came back, he had a woman with him."

"Very good," Hector said. "A beautiful woman, in fact. She spoke perfect New Mexico Spanish. She said she wanted to thank Castillo for his help. Castillo said she must have thought he was the goddam sanctuary movement or something. So he says she's welcome, and he's happy to be such a wonderful guy, and she hands him the other ten. They leave, and Castillo laughs like hell for the rest of the day. He gave the ten-thousand to his drug lieutenants as a bonus."

"Whose crew did he kill?" I asked.

"Well, since you ask," Hector said, "they were mine. Eight guys. Two who brought the group with the Ortegas, two waiting at the house, four more who showed up to take another big group up to Bakersfield. So I owe you again, *amigo*, for helping me find out who did this to my people."

"You don't owe me, Hector. I'm not trying to give anybody a leg up in the drug racket, including you."

"Whatever," he said.

"How come four bodies were at the house and four were on the reservation?" I asked.

"Castillo says Salvador wanted to take all eight and dump them so they could keep using the house for a while. His guys took the first four, but they got nervous and talked him out of dumping the rest. If they got pulled over on the road, they'd have to start shooting cops. That takes things to a whole other level."

"I don't suppose Castillo gave you a name for this guy from California?"

"No," Hector said. "But he did say one other interesting thing. A few days after they made this deal, the guy calls him and asks for something else. Guess what it was?"

The answer clicked into place almost without my thinking about it.

"Following me," I said. "He made that call after he found out that I was hired to investigate the Phoenix killings and two others here."

"Don't know why," Hector said. "I just know what happened. Castillo said he didn't have the manpower for something like that. The guy said okay, he knew some people in East L.A. who owed him. They'd put a few local guys on you. They could rough you up a little, scare you, but not kill you."

"The woman who came along for the payoff," I said. "She didn't know anything about the tail on me?"

"Nope. That was just some side deal the man made. And Castillo forgot about it once he outsourced it."

"Are those East L.A. boys coming after you because of Delgado killing their men?"

"Nah. They'd last thirty seconds down here. They're dumb, but not dumb enough to turn up in the real Mexico."

"Can I talk to Castillo, maybe show him a couple of pictures?"

The line went quiet for a moment. I wondered if our connection had been broken.

"Hector," I said, "can I talk to Castillo?"

"No," Hector said. "He's not gonna be available."

41

Gabi called from La Habra Heights at eight o'clock, exhausted and miserable. A family with two little kids had watched their house burn. Nothing was left but the fireplace, one blackened brick column rising from a half-acre of ashes. If the TV news crews wanted a teddy-bear-in-the-rubble shot, they'd have to bring their own teddy.

Gabi's editor told her to ask the family how they felt.

"If you were in Arizona tonight, I swear I'd have just kept driving," she said. "Go past the fire and stay on the Interstate until the signs said Tucson. And never interview another person in pain again. I know I'm a wimp, but I wish I were there with you and not doing this."

I told her about Rawlins and the coke bust in Vegas. She said she was glad, but fatigue killed the interest in her voice. She gave me the number of her motel in Diamond Bar.

"If I'm too tired to sleep, can I call you at three in the morning and just listen to you talk?" she said.

"Call anytime," I told her. We were comfortably quiet for a while. Finally we said good night. Both us held onto the phone, the way we do when we're apart. I heard hers click first. I hung up and got a beer from the fridge. I stepped onto the balcony, planning to think hard and pull this damn case together. I spent two hours mostly looking absently toward LAX, watching the world's jetliners get out of town.

My cell phone rang at five in the morning.

I looked at the caller ID display, expecting to see Gabi's name. It was Jansson.

"You know what time it is?" I said.

"Imagine how I felt when mine rang at two-thirty," he said.

"What?"

"Late breaking developments," he said. "Come on down."

The address was one of the last remaining old, small office buildings at the Sunset Strip's west end. It looked like Mr. Toad's house. It must have been built even before Kookie was parking cars at the fictional number Seventy-Seven, down the Strip. Most of the boulevard's neon and giant billboards were dark now, but this building was illuminated by the ominous red and blue flashers on police cars.

I parked behind a sheriff's SUV and gave a uniformed deputy my name. He pointed me to the driveway and said Jansson was in the back. I ducked under the yellow tape and squeezed past a crime scene van that filled much of the drive.

Eduardo Salvador's Escalade was in the small rear parking lot, next to a metallic silver Porsche 911 Carrera convertible with the top down. Salvador was in the right seat of the Porsche, slumped forward, with a large bloody mess at the back of his head. A young man in a gray suit, blue shirt, and red silk tie was behind the wheel, leaning against the door. His left eye was closed. His right eye was lost somewhere in the dark crater blown into that side of his skull.

"They made it easy," Jansson said. "Back here in the dark, off the street, nobody around. Hard to believe a hood like Salvador was that stupid."

"Who's the other guy?" I said.

"Thurston K. Gleason, attorney at law," Jansson said. "Thor, his friends called him, apparently because he was really combative in court. He won his last case, all right, but it got him killed. He talked Judge Chin into quashing the Phoenix extradition warrant. Chin's no pushover, either. Gleason walked Salvador out of jail yesterday afternoon. If Eduardo were still in the pokey, these guys would be alive."

"How did they get here?"

"The way we figure it, they went from jail to the impound lot and claimed the Escalade. Salvador has a receipt stamped at four-thirty. Then we figure they came up here to party, have dinner, party some more. Salvador left the Escalade here and they drove off together in the Porsche. Gleason has a bunch of credit card receipts from bars, and one that looks like dinner at a French place a few doors down. Gleason had two-hundred bucks in his pants pocket. Salvador had a little over a thousand. I'm a senior detective, so I was able to rule out robbery."

"Why this lot?" I said. "I counted four 'no parking' signs between here and the street."

"Gleason rents a space," Jansson said. "We called the owner. He says Gleason parks here every day because his own office building has no parking. It was cool with the owner if Gleason let a friend or two park here at night."

"So," I said, "somebody followed them here and watched them drive off in the Porsche to wherever they went. He knew they'd be back around the time the bars close, so Salvador could pick up his Escalade."

"Two a.m. That's what we figure. And the coroner says that looks pretty good for time of death."

"Who found them?"

"Teenage couple. They pulled in here for a little smooching or whatever. Give 'em credit, they called it right in. Lot of kids would have thrown up and raced out of here."

"Can I get close for a minute?"

"Hands off the cars, but you can go beside them for a look."

I moved carefully between the Porsche and the Escalade. The front bumper of the big Cadillac was a yard or so from the wall at the back of the lot. There was no other structure behind the wall, just a hill with houses at the top. The angle was almost straight up. Nobody in the houses could have seen much down here.

"The shooter waits in front of the Escalade," I said. "The Porsche comes up, stops, the shooter jumps out. Two quick steps, he'd be right at the Porsche's door. Salvador gets it first, because he's the target, he's closer, and he's the one more likely to have a gun. Then the shooter pops the lawyer before the poor devil can even react."

"You should do this for a living," Jansson said.

"Then the killer just strolls off to his own car somewhere in the neighborhood. I'll bet he left the gun."

"Thrown under the Porsche. We ran it. Stolen from Whittier a month ago. The theft report is legit. The owner is a 62-year-old librarian who happens to be aunt to a sergeant on the Whittier force. He taught her how to shoot. No other prints on it."

I stepped away from the cars and wandered around the small lot. I looked down the driveway to Sunset. Morning rush hour was underway. Traffic was building up in both directions.

"You know," I said, "we're only three or four blocks from José Liebowitz's place."

"And only three or four miles from the Sharon Tate house," Jansson said. "And John Belushi, he checked out at the Chateau Marmont, just down Sunset."

"Quite a coincidence, though."

"Not really, Brinker. I've worked a lot of cases up here. Plenty of people died ugly in this neighborhood."

"A pro did José," I said. "This was a pro, for sure."

Jansson sighed. "Brilliant," he said. "I'm pretty certain we only have one professional killer in L.A. Had to be the same guy did these poor devils and José. Sure."

We stood there, staring at the bodies, then looking up the hill to the precariously perched houses, then at each other.

"Starbucks down the Strip ought to be open," Jansson said. "Let's take a walk, get a cup."

We hiked east on a hilly stretch of Sunset. The air felt cool and heavy. The sky was morning L.A. gray. Cars idled, bumper to bumper, waiting at red lights and left turn lanes.

At the coffee shop, Jansson surprised me by doing the grande half-caf, fat-free milk foam routine with the barista. I ordered a latte with a double shot. I paid for both and didn't get much change for a ten. We sat at a tiny corner table, away from the customer lines.

"These murders, the Phoenix house, they're all tied in somehow," I said.

"Why?" Jansson asked.

"I'm the connection," I said. "I'm investigating Liebowitz's murder, and I was onto Salvador for the Phoenix killings."

"Why?" he said.

"What do you mean, why?"

"Why were you onto Salvador? I know you were investigating Liebowitz because Carla hired you. But why Salvador?"

"Phoenix cops put his name out on the murders at that immigrant house," I said.

"I know that. I saw the warrant. I told you, remember? Why were you on that case in the first place?"

"Because Carla was afraid that clients of hers might have been victims there. She had lost two, Liebowitz and Bergstrom, the berry grower up in Camarillo. So she wanted me to look at all three cases."

Jansson looked at me over the top of his cup. His face was red. I didn't think it was from the coffee.

"Clients of hers?" he said. "They were illegals who just arrived."

"She thought one of them might have been a woman who contacted her about coming up from Mexico."

"Brinker," Jansson said, "I ought to haul your ass down to the jail right now. I'm sitting here with two unsolved 187's. Something doesn't happen on one of these pretty quick, I look like an idiot. And you've been holding out on me."

"Holding out what? I don't know anything."

"You know Carla Baca is mixed up in this mess, somehow."

"I don't know that," I said. "She could just be at the edge of it, not doing anything wrong. Just entangled somehow."

"Entangled is good," Jansson said. "I like entangled. I'll take entangled because I don't have shit on Liebowitz and I'm not real optimistic about this new one."

He shook his head. He took a deep breath and exhaled noisily through his lips like a tired old plow horse.

"When I was just a little boy, my mother said, 'Son, don't ever trust a P.I.' I should have listened to her."

"I bought the coffee," I said. "And the ice cream at Farmers Market. How bad can I be?"

"Okay, that's a mitigating factor," he said. "So redeem yourself. You got any idea who took Señor Salvador off the board?"

"I think that job would have had a whole bunch of applicants," I said.

"Well, from what I saw of him, I'd say it was a public service. But I don't need a squad of civic-minded marksmen running around, making personal decisions about who stays and who goes. You know?"

"I know," I said.

"Share that knowledge with anyone who could use it." He stood. "Let's go. We both have work to do. I need to talk to my boss, and to yours, too."

"She's not my boss any more," I said. "She said goodbye and keep the change."

"Then you can tell her without fear of reprisal that she needs to lay it all out for me. Everything. Otherwise, I'll make her the sorriest lawyer in L.A."

"Except Thor," I said.

"Well, yeah," Jansson said. "Except for him."

And I still hadn't mentioned Richard Rawlins.

42

I drove back to the marina. The double shot left me wired but still tired after my abbreviated sleep. Los Angeles rush hour traffic ran both ways. I headed out of town, moving no faster than the drones driving in. Tucson was looking better by the day, except that Gabi was not there.

Baseball had just passed the All Star break. The American League won again. Sportscasters talked about home run totals and ERA's and batting averages. I was hitting .333. The Ortegas were safe at their new home, although illegally, and Salvador was out of the game for good. None of that was my doing, but I gave myself credit anyway. I had two strikeouts. José Liebowitz and Bo Bergstrom.

I scrambled three eggs and toasted two slices of bread. I put a big spoonful of Gabi's homemade salsa next to the eggs. I poured a glass of orange juice. I ate. I drank. When I finished, I cleaned up the kitchen. All this motion allowed me to feel busy without actually thinking about the case and failing, again, to figure out anything.

The only clues pointing to Rawlins were the cocaine charge in Vegas and the ID by José's neighbor. Maybe more web snooping would help. I couldn't do that, though. Gabi had taken her laptop to the fire. Mine was home in Tucson.

Then I remembered another computer. I ran downstairs to the apartment parking lot. José Liebowitz's laptop and date book were in the trunk of my car. His sister gave them to me when I visited her in Riverside. The Ortega problem had become so consuming that I forgot about the computer. It seemed unimportant. I assumed that the sheriff's detectives went over the files before releasing it to Sandra Liebowitz Brown.

I opened the white case and pushed the "on" button. This might be a futile effort. José probably had a password, and Gabi told me how she struggled to rig up her wireless home network with security. I got lucky. The machine booted up without demanding a password. José was careless, but his corner-cutting might help me now.

The electronic desktop appeared. A striking portrait of Carla Baca filled the screen, the picture from the "Beauty of Immigration Law" magazine article. Poor José. The lonely guy, dreaming of the lovely unattainable lawyer who wanted him only as a client.

I dropped the cursor to the bottom of the screen. A horizontal row of program icons popped up. I clicked on the calendar and backed up to May, when Liebowitz had been murdered. He had entered no appointments or reminders for May 14, the day of his death. I found no entry in the paper appointment book, either.

I found another icon for the address book. José had dozens of names with contact information listed. Carla's office, of course, and Norton Silber, the attorney-accountant. About half the contacts included email addresses with the .mx suffix. I figured those were clients from Mexico. Several were offices with the word *musica* in their names. Bo Bergstrom was not in the address book. Neither was Richard Rawlins or anyone with a similar name.

Dead end.

A couple of years before, I had been hired to find a sixteen-year-old runaway named Carrie Dahlman. She left no obvious clue. Her boyfriend was as baffled as anyone. Her girlfriends weren't talking. Carrie's parents gave me permission to turn her bedroom inside out. Nothing, but I wondered about her computer. When I struck out with that, I called the Alejandro & Katz information technology consultant, a cheerful geek named Charlie Bivens. Charlie spent five minutes doing whatever those guys do, then gave me a printout and big smug grin.

The printout listed two of Carrie's friends, unknown to her parents, with addresses and phone numbers. Their emails had stanford.edu addresses. I found Carrie in Palo Alto, California the next day. She was drinking coffee near the Stanford campus with two football players and a girl whose name was in that hidden computer file.

So, with José Liebowitz's computer in front of me, I called Charlie again.

"Brinker!" he said. He has a voice like one of those squeaky little characters in video games. "Back on the trail of pubescent hotties?"

"I wish," I said. "Charlie, if I want to find a guy's contacts and appointments that he doesn't enter in the address book and calendar, where do I look?"

"Is this a pro or your basic computer user?"

"Basic, I imagine."

"Well, then," Charlie said, "he's probably a pushover. What kind of computer?"

"A white laptop," I said.

"I don't care about the color," Charlie said, laughing. He's the kind of guy who can laugh at you and not make you mad. "That sounds like an older Mac, though."

"It says iBook G4."

"Ah, I'm right again. Have you found the dock? You know what a dock is? Move the cursor down the bottom and a bunch of icons should appear."

"Got it," I said.

"Okay. Is there blue 'W' on there?"

"Yes."

"Excellent. Click it."

I did. In a moment, the word processor appeared on the screen.

"Okay."

"Now, look up on the top left," Charlie said. "You should see an icon that looks like a file folder with a little arrow on it. Click that."

"All right. Now I've got a long list of documents."

"Ah, you're a high tech whiz, Brinker. Now here's how it usually works. Most of the file names are obvious and truthful, like 'Letter to idiot airline that lost my bags.' So you're looking for something that obviously identifies what you want, like 'Secret stuff.'"

"You're joking," I said.

"You'd be amazed at the things I see. Anyhow, it could also be a file name that seems to mean nothing. Tell me what you've got."

I scrolled down the list. All the file names looked legit. Many began with "Contract," then had the name of a person or group. A couple said, "Note to Sandra" and "Note to Sandra 2." There were items he apparently downloaded from news sites and pasted into the word processor. Then I came to one titled simply "R."

"Here's one that doesn't have any meaning on the surface, but it might be the initial of somebody I'm worried about," I said.

"Betcha that's it," Charlie said.

I clicked. A little dialog box popped up. It read, "Enter password to open file."

"Uh-oh," I said.

"Password protected, eh?"

"Yeah."

"Well, if I had the machine right here with me, I could probably crack it pretty fast. For now, though, you'll have to guess."

"Wonderful," I said.

"No, no. Be optimistic. If this computer owner were smart, he'd choose some random combination of letters and numbers, gibberish when you see it. But luckily for me, and today for you, most computer users are not smart. If this guy has a dog, try entering the name or breed. You know, like 'Spot' or 'weiner dog' or something. That works about half the time."

"No dog," I said.

"Hmm. He might have had one as a child. You probably don't know that, though. Okay. Next best bet is his own kid's name."

"No kids," I said.

"Lucky him," Charlie said.

"Not really," I said.

"Oh. Well, does he have a girl friend or a boy friend?"

I typed in "Carla" and hit the OK button.

"Charlie," I said, "you're a genius."

"But am I well adjusted and socially adept?" he said, laughing again.

"For a man in your field. Thanks, pal."

"*De nada, amigo*," he said. The phone clicked off.

The "R" file was not big. The first item was a phone number with a 310 area code. Somewhere on the west side of Los Angeles, maybe Santa Monica or Westwood or part of Beverly Hills. I felt certain that it was Richard Rawlins's cell phone.

Several lines listed a date, a time, and R. The last line said, "May 14, 9 pm, R. Need $1K."

May 14 was the date that José Liebowitz had been shot to death.

I punched star-six-seven on my cell phone to block my number from Caller ID. I called R's phone. I was holding my breath by the fourth ring. Voice mail kicked in. "This is Richard Rawlins," his recorded voice said, then gave the leave-a-message spiel.

I didn't have enough for a prosecutor, but it was plenty to take to Carla. I called her office. Amric came on.

"Mister Brinker," he said, "Carla is not in at present, but I expect her this afternoon."

"I need to see her right away, Amric. Where is she?"

He thought for a moment. Apparently he decided that I was on Carla's team.

"She went to collect Mister Rawlins," he said. "The firefighters in La Habra Heights have two helicopters out of service because of mechanical difficulty. Mister Rawlins often allows them to use his in emergencies. He flew there and Carla has driven out to meet him."

I called Jansson but got no answer. I left a message telling him where I was going and why. He wouldn't think it was much, but he might come out to ask some questions and see what happened.

43

The firefighters worked from a command post at Hacienda Park. It was a lucky location, with a big parking lot for equipment and a community building to house catering, rest, and first aid services.

The guard told me that helicopters were landing at a clearing next to the boulevard, about a mile north. He called a chief on the two-way and said I was there to see Rawlins. The chief had better things to do than argue, so he told the guard to send me up. The guard gave me a pass for my windshield and pointed me north.

"Stay alert up there, sir," he said. "It's calm now, but you never know what the wind will do."

Rawlins's helicopter, rotors turning, was on a dusty lot across the boulevard from a hillside thick with brush. Utility crews had dug their poles out of the ground and restrung power lines low at the west perimeter, effectively doubling the chopper landing and liftoff area. An orange windsock was planted near the road, registering almost no breeze.

Way above us, across the highway, California ranch houses on big lots fanned out across a hilltop plateau. A fire crew worked at the bottom of the hill, stomping through blackened shrubs where the flames had been beaten down.

I saw four men in the chopper, all in firefighting gear, none of them Rawlins. The helicopter rose very slowly and climbed at the angle of the hillside, keeping a steady fifty feet or so from the surface.

It was plainly an observation flight to give commanders a view of any smoldering hot spots on the hill. Every so often, the bright blue R-44 hovered, then rotated 180 degrees in place, so passengers on both sides could have a good look at the treacherous hill. It seemed risky to me, swinging the tail boom around so close to the hillside. The pilot was a pro, though, as good as I had seen on the Border Patrol. As smooth as Rawlins, or better.

A deputy sheriff stopped me just below the staging area. He looked at my pass and pointed to the hilltop.

"Mister Rawlins is up on Leucadia, watching from the high ground," he said. "A lady picked him up in her Lexus about a half hour ago. I can't let you through here, sir. We need to keep the boulevard clear for fire equipment. You'll have to return to the command post, take a right, and go up the back way." He pulled a piece of paper from a clipboard and drew a crude map of the neighborhood streets.

I found myself on a steep, twisty road called Ardsheal. It ended at Skyline Drive, near the very top of the Heights. I took Skyline east to Hacienda Boulevard. Another deputy saw the pass in my windshield and waved me across to Leucadia. A Lexus sedan was parked at an overlook. Carla and Rawlins stood beside the car, looking down on the firefighters and the scorched hills.

They turned around as I pulled in beside their car. Carla looked surprised to see me. Rawlins looked unhappy.

"Amric told me where to find you," I said.

"What is it?" Carla said.

I looked at Rawlins and said, "Game's over, Rich."

He stood impassively, looking first at me, then at Carla. He was dressed for the outdoors, in jeans and a short sleeve T-shirt. If he carried a weapon, I couldn't see it.

Carla said to me, "What are you talking about, Brinker?"

"José Liebowitz had Rich's phone number in a personal file," I said. "They met on the night Liebowitz died. Rich was José's cocaine connection. That was Rich's way of getting close enough to kill him."

I don't know what I expected from Carla. Maybe incredulity, shouting that I was crazy, that this was impossible. Maybe a sobbing collapse. I underestimated her, though. She stood up straight and stared down Rawlins as though he were a courtroom witness of uncertain reliability.

She turned to me and said, "Why in the world would Rich want to kill José?"

"For you," I said.

"Not for me," she snapped. "I would never want such a thing, let alone ask that it be done."

"You missed my point, Carla," I said. "He did it to eliminate a rival."

"A rival? A romantic rival, you mean? That's ridiculous. I never had that kind of interest in José." She was about to say something more, but then she realized the other implication of what I had told her. She turned again to Rawlins, but could not speak.

Rawlins said, "The guy was always hanging around. Some small time talent agent thought he was worthy of you. I saw that he wasn't. What a pathetic jerk he was. I bought his trust with a little coke and a sympathetic ear. When he said you were the only real woman he ever met, I knew he wouldn't leave you alone. So I acted. I was protecting you, Carla."

The helicopter was opposite the top of the hill now, maybe a hundred yards south of us. The pilot turned east, moving toward the next ravine to be inspected. The wind came up, rustling the tops of the eucalyptus trees. The copter swayed a bit, but seemed to be well under control.

Carla kept her gaze on Rawlins. When she spoke, it was only one word, choked out through tears.

"Bo?" she said.

"Bo," Rawlins said, sneering it. "A farmer. And you were sneaking up there to hick country to sleep with him. You weren't fooling anybody, Carla. I couldn't let you keep making that mistake. You would have been miserable with a man like that."

"My father sold insurance to men like that," Carla said. "He drove hundreds of miles to see them in Belen and Hatch and Las Cruces. Even when he had nothing to sell, he'd just go to visit their farms and ranches. He said they were some of the best men in the world."

Rawlins went on as if she hadn't spoken. The scene was eerily like a couple of lawyers, presenting their factual summations. Rawlins did not look or sound like a crazy person. He believed himself.

"Your father caved the first time he ran into trouble," he said. "He and people like him couldn't play in this league."

If Carla had any affection left for the man, it died with those words. She stood there, unable to speak, staring at a man she had thought she knew.

Rawlins said, "You told me he always worked late by himself on Tuesday nights. So I just went up there on a Tuesday night, made sure nobody else was around, and walked into the office. Those yokels don't even any security, not a bit. A man like that would never have protected you."

It was enough, but I had to finish it so Carla would know how badly she had been betrayed.

"And those eight men in Phoenix," I said. "You used Castillo in Nogales to hire Salvador, and he had them all killed."

She raised her hands to her face and gasped. She staggered back and braced herself against her car.

"Oh, dear God," she said. "I did that with him. We did that together."

"I don't think so, Carla," I said. "You and he arranged a guardian angel for Lourdes Ortega and her family. But it was Rich who told Castillo that he didn't care what happened to any of the people involved. Salvador could have killed everyone but the Ortegas. That would have been fine with Rich."

"But I was there when we paid off Castillo," she said. "You saw us that day in Nogales. There was nothing said about killing people."

"Nothing you knew of," I said.

The wind grew unsettled. Gusts swept across the hilltop, then quickly dropped away to dead calm. I saw the chopper swerve and bounce in the unpredictable air currents. It swung closer to the hillside. I wished the pilot would get it out of the canyon and safely onto the ground.

"Where did you get this supposed information?" Rawlins said.

"Castillo explained it all to some people I know," I said. The light seemed to go out of Rawlins's eyes. He knew what kind of people played in Castillo's league. He knew what happened without being told.

"Right after Carla hired me, you put the tails on me, Rich. And two of them got killed because somebody else was watching them."

Carla said, "Twelve people, Rich. Twelve people."

"Nothing people, every one of them," Rawlins said. "Lowlifes and losers."

I heard a car behind me. Rawlins was looking over my shoulder. I turned and saw Jansson approaching in his unmarked sedan. Someone was with him. When I turned back to Carla and Rawlins, I saw the helicopter behind them, descending, trying line up a straight approach to the landing zone.

Rawlins grabbed Carla's hand and backed up to the edge of the plateau.

"The helicopter will be waiting at the bottom of the hill, Carla," he said. "Let's get out of here. Leave Brinker and his cop friend to discuss their conspiracy theories."

"No," Carla said.

"Come on, Carla!" Rawlins shouted.

Jansson had pulled into the overlook. He and a man in full firefighter gear got out of the car.

"Now, Carla!" Rawlins said.

She tried to stand her ground, but couldn't tear his hand from his grip. He started down the hillside, pulling her. The ground was steep, not sheer. No path marked the way down, but they could scramble through the brush to the helicopter landing area with no danger of a bad fall.

I started after them. A gust of wind, the strongest yet, kicked up a cloud of dust from the dry earth of the overlook. When I saw them again, Carla was struggling, trying to hit Rawlins with her free hand. Behind them, the helicopter moved side to side and bounced down through the choppy air, toward the landing area.

Behind me, atop the hill, Jansson stood with a gun in his hand. No chance of a shot. The firefighter was shouting and gesturing frantically with his arm in a way that meant, "Come back." I went forward, down the hill, after Rawlins and Carla.

They had twenty yards on me. One man moving freely should be able to close the distance on another man dragging a captive down. I felt confident until a rock slipped from under my foot and sent me sprawling face first. It knocked the wind out of me. I rose just in time to see Carla, still in Rawlins's grasp, throw herself against his legs. His knees buckled. He lost his grip on Carla and fell. Carla scrambled up toward me.

For a moment, I lost sight of Rawlins. He must have fallen at a spot where the hill dropped sharply for a few feet. Then I saw him rolling downhill. He went twenty yards before he stopped on a patch of flat ground. He stood, looking shaky. He was halfway to the road now. He saw his helicopter hover, then settle softly on the landing area. He started down.

Carla reached me. I tried to pull her up but she jerked her hand away. The firefighter who had arrived with Jansson had worked his way down to us. He reached under Carla's arms from behind, like a lifeguard in deep water, and pulled her along as he backed up the hill. He was a powerful man and Carla looked like a rag doll in his rescuing embrace.

Rawlins neared the boulevard. The fire crews had beaten down flames there, but from my elevated vantage point, I saw hotspots smoking. Near the road, a eucalyptus tree bent at the crown. At the landing zone, the windsock went from limp to pointing in my direction.

I heard a harsh rushing noise unlike anything I ever heard in nature before.

At that moment, the smoking spots on the lower hillside erupted in fire, as if a dozen gas wells had been punctured. Flames shot high and wide, filling my vision. Even at my distance, the oxygen seemed to be sucked out of the air.

Rawlins must have screamed as he died, but his cries were lost in the roar of the blinding fireballs.

EPILOGUE

I did not speak to Carla Baca again until September, when she sent me a plane ticket to Mazatlán. She met me at a beachfront hotel called the Balboa Club. Her hair had grown. She pulled it back in a ponytail. She wore lightweight tan slacks, a pink cotton blouse, and white walking shoes that looked barely used. She could have been any successful lawyer taking early retirement or a long vacation in Mexico. She was not rested or relaxed, though. She looked exhausted and tense. That Carla sparkle was nowhere in sight.

The sun blistered the beach, even as fall neared. We sat at a little table in the indoor bar, looking south toward town.

"You could probably turn things around if you came back," I said. "Nobody's after you. I think you could still practice."

"It's a privilege," she said. "I don't deserve it."

"I talked to David Katz, the lawyer I work for in Tucson," I said. "He says that you didn't do anything to get disbarred for. You didn't personally break any laws or literally encourage lawbreaking. The people who told you they were crossing the border would have crossed anyway, no matter what you said."

"I used horrible judgment," she said.

"Maybe aiding and abetting on Lourdes and her family, but David says that could be handled. Drop the charges for a little community service."

"How could a client trust me?" Carla said. "How could other lawyers or a court trust me?"

"You got fooled by a guy who loved you. He lost his way and dragged you along," I said. "It's not the first time that happened to a smart woman."

She shook her head.

"I'm not going back," she said. "Not to California and not to law."

A vendor walked up the beach. He was just a kid, maybe eleven or twelve, lugging a big bag on his shoulder. I knew by the lumpy shape that the bag was filled with canned drinks and ice. It probably weighed thirty pounds. The boy said something to a tourist couple lying on beach towels, roasting their plump bodies in the sun. They waved him away as if he were a beggar in a souk.

Carla said, "Did he suffer, do you think?"

"Who?" I asked. "There's been plenty of suffering."

"Rich," she said. "At the end, in the fire."

"Probably not," I said. "I saw something on TV a few days ago. Apparently they use volunteer kids from reform school, whatever they call it now, they use these kids to fight fires. Years ago, some of them were doing mop-up at a fire scene. They got caught by a huge gust of winds. The wind can turn embers into a monster fire, I guess. The coroner said the kids were probably knocked unconscious by the fire blast and the lack of oxygen. Never knew what hit them."

Brinker, the kindly liar.

Carla couldn't look at me as I told her this. She stared into the vague distance, perhaps calculating her own culpability in each awful moment from José Liebowitz's murder to Rawlins's failed trial by fire on the hillside.

"Bo might have been the one," she said. "A decent man, kind. Didn't care about the L.A. glitz. But Rich was charming and fun and close by, and willing to do anything I asked. So I trusted the wrong guy and got the right guy killed."

"Way too hard on yourself, Carla."

"He knew about my father. All that time, he knew about Daddy. Mom and I never told a soul when we came to Tucson. I told myself I'd become a fighter, try to get some justice for people like us. I wonder what Rich would have said if I told him someday. Probably lie and say he had no idea."

I thought of the moment Rawlins lost her forever. The moment when he spoke ill of her father.

"I asked you to come for just one thing," she said. "I want to look you in the eye and tell you that I never meant harm. I wasn't trying to lie to you, even though I did about Lourdes Ortega. I just reached that point where everything was getting out of control. I tried to save the situation and made it worse. But I never meant to wrong anyone. That includes you."

"You could have told me this on the phone," I said.

"No, I couldn't. I have to say it to your face. I want to have at least a shred of integrity left. I've hurt people. I can't just blow them off and say 'sorry' on the phone."

The waiter came by and poured more coffee. It was strong and smooth. It reminded me of something I wanted to do.

"If you need anything from the firm," Carla said, "call Amric. When I sold the practice, part of the deal was that Amric becomes a shareholder when he passes the bar. He should be admitted this fall."

"Where will you go?" I said.

"San Miguel de Allende," she said. "Rich had a place there."

"I remember. He said he was always trying to get you there."

"It's beautiful. Cobblestone streets and lovely old houses. Lots of Americans live there, but not enough to ruin it completely yet. Rich left his house to me. I don't need to work."

"Maybe not to earn money," I said. "But you can't just go to expatriate cocktail parties for the rest of your life."

"I know. I'll take a little time and figure out something worthwhile to do."

"You don't need a lifetime of penance and exile," I said. "You might do the most good by doing the work you're good at. By going home."

"I never really thought that Albuquerque or Tucson was home," she said. "I thought Los Angeles was, because I made my own way there. But I blew it. Where's home when you blow it?" She stared out to sea.

The tourist couple, red-faced, walked quickly in our direction, seeking beer and air conditioning. The young vendor had turned around and trudged back along the beach to the next hotel.

"You know what some magazine in Mexico called me once?" she asked.

"*Nuestra señora del norte*," I said.

"Yes." She shook her head. "How pathetic is that?"

"Goodbye, Carla," I said.

"I am sorry," she said.

I felt her eyes on my back as I walked out to the taxi stand. Riding back to the airport, I had the driver stop at a *supermercado* on the frontage road. I asked the manager for advice. He walked me to the correct aisle and pointed out his favorites. He said I spoke good Spanish. I didn't tell him about my years of practice on the Border Patrol. I bought five pounds of fine coffee from Oaxaca and another five from Chiapas, close to Guatemala.

Gabi said, "I left a CD in your car. Mark Knopfler and Emmylou Harris. Like the man said, there's a lot of wisdom in country music, Brinker."

"Thanks," I said. I kissed the top of her head and held her tight.

"If you get to Yuma and think about turning around," she said, "do it. I won't change the locks. Remember what I told you that night. You're home now. Here."

She stood on her tiptoes and put her hands behind my neck and pulled my face to hers. We kissed for a long but too short time. She said, "You better go, or you'll never get to Tucson. I'll never get to work.

"How would we pass the hours?" I said.

"Go," she said.

The first cut on the CD was called "Beachcombing." I was on the 405 when I played it. It sounded like a song about hurricane wreckage, but another meaning emerged as they got into it. Mark carried the lyric, resigned to personal damage. Emmylou hit a high, mournful counterpoint on the chorus. Despite its sadness, the song had a perfect rhythm for the freeway: gently up-tempo, moving steadily ahead, nothing frantic.

When it ended, I pushed the backtrack button to hear it again. I pictured the eight-hour ride down through San Diego and over to Tucson. Five-hundred miles from Gabi. I watched the exit signs come up, Slauson and La Cienega, Century and Imperial. How many miles back to the marina?

Emmylou sang, "Head on home."

AUTHOR'S NOTE

The Center for Latin American and Border Studies at New Mexico State University has provided valuable information for me, as it does for everyone interested in border issues. The center's Frontera NorteSur offers online coverage of news events on both sides of the United States border with Mexico. Its Internet address is http://www.nmsu.edu/~frontera/

"*Aeromigrante*" airlines really did fly. I learned about them from a news report by Chris Hawley of the Arizona Republic's Mexico City bureau.

Gabi's "bread knife weather" book was *Briarpatch* by Ross Thomas.

I am grateful to the following generous people for their help with aviation information, law, and lore: My good friend Commander Chuck Street, well-known to television and radio audiences for his helicopter reports in Los Angeles; Henry Austin of the Robinson Helicopter Company in Torrance, California; and Jo Ann Wilson of AOPA, the Aircraft Owners and Pilots Association, in Frederick, Maryland.

When I gave Richard Rawlins his helicopter, nobody had registered its number, N187RR, with the Federal Aviation Administration. Therefore, any resemblance to actual aircraft, owners, or pilots really is purely coincidental.

ABOUT THE AUTHOR

James C. Mitchell's first two novels featuring the Tucson private investigator Brinker were nominated for Shamus Awards by the Private Eye Writers of America.

Mitchell teaches news media law and other subjects in the University of Arizona School of Journalism. He has worked as a broadcast reporter and anchor in New York City, Los Angeles, and for seventeen years in Louisville, Kentucky. He was a prosecutor in Mohave County, Arizona.

He divides his time between Tucson and Colorado.

http://www.jamescmitchell.net

www.ingramcontent.com/pod-product-compliance
Lightning Source LLC
Chambersburg PA
CBHW031322170626
46807CB00002B/526